A DUCK TO WATER

G. B. Stern

Illustrated by Sarah Chamberlin Scott

J. N. TOWNSEND PUBLISHING
EXETER, NEW HAMPSHIRE
2004

First Printing

Published by

J. N. Townsend Publishing
4 Franklin Street
Exeter, New Hampshire 03833
Townsendpub@aol.com
www.jntownsendpublishing.com
1-800-333-9883
603-778-9883
Fax: 603-772-1980

Library of Congress Cataloging-in-Publication Data
Stern, G. B. (Gladys Bronwyn), 1890-
A duck to water / by G. B. Stern.
p. cm.
1. Ducklings—fiction. 2. Difference (Psychology)—
Fiction. I. Title.
PR6037.T453 D83 2002
823'.912—dc21   2001057004

ISBN: 1-880158-40-X

A Duck to Water

"From troubles of the world
I turn to ducks, . . .

"When God had finished the stars and whirl of coloured suns
He turned His mind from big things to fashion little ones,
Beautiful tiny things (like daisies) He made, and then
He made the comical ones in case the minds of men
Should stiffen and become
Dull, humourless and glum:
And so forgetful of their Maker be
As to take even themselves—quite seriously."
—F.W. HARVEY, *Ducks.*

"The ducks say '*Why* can't fellows be allowed to do *what* they like *when* they like and *as* they like, instead of other fellows sitting on banks and watching them all the time and making remarks and poetry and things about them? What *nonsense* it all is!' That's what the ducks say."

"So it is, so it is," said the Mole with great heartiness.

"No, it isn't!" cried the Rat indignantly.

"Well, then, it isn't, it isn't," replied the Mole soothingly.

—KENNETH GRAHAME, *The Wind in the Willows.*

Prologue

HOLLY, THAT BEASTLY, BEAUTIFUL CAT, lay in her basket, a laconic mother, with her seething mass of nine silver kittens all blindly trying to oust one another in such closeness of union with their parent as since their actual birth could no longer be achieved. Holly suffered it because for the moment it suited her temperament. Directly she wished to slink out at night and be over the wall of the garden, free and a huntress once more, no amount of kittens would keep her back. Meanwhile she felt a little languid; languid and conceited. After all, *nine*—

"*Nine!*" exclaimed a chorus of enthusiastic voices, standing above her lying-in basket. "My dear, it's *too* wonderful! Nine! I've never seen as many all together like that! It's a phenomenon! And all different shades of silver like a shoal of mackerel—no, sardines. And isn't Holly sweet with them! Look, she's a perfect mother!"

Holly yawned and closed her eyes; little ripples passed down her close-fitting dark-grey plush coat. These Visitor Legs! And then her own adoring Legs, privileged to take charge of her and attend to her supply department, replied excitedly to a Visitor Legs who had apparently never been to Brambleford before: "Oh no, it's not her first litter. She's had one lot of three, and then two, and once five, and—let's see—two and one and one and the last litter was four (I don't believe you say "litter" for cats)—But never *nine.*"

"And all silver! Have you any idea who—?"

"Not the faintest. All kinds have been simply flocking; they always do. There was a large ginger, and a black with a white chest and white paws, and several Tom-tabs—common, but quite nice markings. In fact, I thought Holly preferred one of the tabs, but you never know."

"If only she could talk," babbled an impulsive Visitor Legs, "she'd tell us."

That's all you know, Holly reflected; could, yes; would, no. "Why should I?" She did not suffer nitwits gladly. Nevertheless, though she was already bursting with swank before they came to pay her this visit of congratulation (summoned no doubt by her own Legs), their wonder and incredulity sustained her pride, and she offered no objection even when a squirming kitten was picked out and held for a moment out of her reach, though her eyes grew anxious till it was restored to her and she was able by frantic licking to rid it quickly of that unpleasant smell of human fingers, and what was there to laugh at in that? But then you could not expect any Legs to have a sense of humour. Now the father of the nine was by far the wittiest of her motley collection of lovers. It's a wise kitten, he had said, breaking down a couple of early daffodils in his ardour, it's a wise kitten—now how did it go on? Holly had forgotten; how could you possibly think in such a crowd? Still, she would not have wanted even one less than nine. Nine was really such a distinguished kindle. Probably no cat had ever before had as many.

The Visitor Legs were leaving now, still on a high admiring note, one of them rushing back twice and flinging herself down beside the basket—"just for another wee peep at the angel little bundles of silver," she explained.

Nine!

A week later:

"Eleven! My dear, *no!* And all black? All of them? Eleven!"

Holly shook off those nine little pests that would never leave her alone, and sprang from her basket. The conversations of her Legs on the telephone were usually never of the slightest interest except when she described Holly's beauty and intelligence (both undeniable), her charm and affectionate nature (both non-existent). But what she was saying now compelled attention, though from Holly's point of view almost too bad to be true: "Eleven! . . . Good Heavens! . . . Yes, of course you were right to ring me at once! . . . I never heard of so many before, not all in one what-do-you-call-it! . . . Yes, I'll be round at once, the moment I've finished my weeding. I simply can't wait to see the wuffie-itsie-bitsie-sweets. I shan't believe it till I see them! *Eleven!*"

Holly went forth at once, leaving her measly nine at their forlorn seeking of what was no longer there; and as a logical vent to spite and rage, killed a young thrush whom she was lucky enough to find accessible and unprotected—except, of course, by an ineffectual mother thrush.

One

ELEVEN BLACK DUCKLINGS, however lovable, were bound to be a shock to the mothering hen, who naturally had not expected anything quite so absurd to emerge from the dim warm eggs that had somehow come to mean so much to her during the long days and weeks they had been left undisturbed in the straw of the hen-house. When the Feeding Legs came across the bridge from the garden to the meadow to feed the ducks and the hens and the geese, rattling the corn in the saucepan, the brown mother-hen still would not leave her eggs, no, not for all the corn in the world; the Feeding Legs had to come into the hen-house and sprinkle a few grains to tempt her off.

"She's a good one, that," said the Feeding Legs in hearty approbation. "They aren't all such good mothers. Nothing like. That other one isn't, in the next box." For a sister of the brown hen had also had that queer urge . . . "Broody," the Feeding Legs called it, but of course it was nothing dowdy and scruffy like that; just an inexplicable longing to remain quietly at home and squat in a sort of dream: "No, thanks, I don't want anything to eat. No, thanks, I don't feel like laying. No, thanks, I'd rather not go out; it's my own affair if I shed my feathers, isn't it? And it's no use bringing me gossip about my husband, I'm not interested. Besides, roosters will be roosters. I can't settle to anything . . . I just want to be left alone." So they left her alone, and her prettier sister too, in the next-door box, Rhoda with the red-gold feathers; until, about two mornings ago, the Feeding Legs had exclaimed: "Why, Rhoda's beaten you to it, after all! Five, and one born dead; well, that's not too bad."

Five lively little packets of yellow fluff; five greedy squeaking little chickens opening and shutting their pointed beaks in a desperate hurry to be fed and to grow and be fed again, and again, and again. The Feeding Legs and her husband, the Stable Legs, were very pleased. They took them in a basket across the plank bridge and into the Garden and the Cottage, for the Owner Legs to see them. The Nitwit Legs, who had only lately come to stay and who belonged to the town, asked at once which were boys and which were

2

girls? And the Stable Legs replied good-humouredly: "You're expecting too much, Miss. We won't be able to tell for a while yet which is pullets and which cockerels. We're hoping they'll mostly be pullets."

"Not but that the cocky-boys have their uses, too," put in the Feeding Legs, relishing a secret of some gruesome significance.

Pullets. Cockerels. Mysterious terms which hovered always over life in the Meadow, and seemed to control the population's comings and goings; they had never quite been able to sort it out for themselves. Meanwhile, Rhoda paraded her chickens in front of her quiet brown sister-hen, and called her a slowcoach and a lazybones. But that did not matter; the comfortable dream went on.

Beneath her were strange little sounds and stirrings; all was not as quiet as it had been before; then a shell cracked; and another shell,—tough shells, tougher than seemed perfectly right . . . and hours went by . . . and the brown hen was never able to remember the exact moment when a vague premonition seized her. She was a reserved little soul and confided in no one. And things were happening too fast now to reverse time and go back to those joyous April mornings before even the blossom was out. But . . . what was this brood, greyish black, with long narrow heads and webbed mackintosh feet and flat hard protruding beaks? Beaks squawking with all their might, grotesque and yet appealing—Could they be chickens, one day to grow into hens like herself? Could they indeed be the result of that long unbroken vigilance, crouching deep in the straw to keep life warm?

"Well," thought the brown hen, sorely bewildered, "no good pretending that it's very satisfactory, and I hope the Legs won't be too disappointed and call it my fault, because I'm sure I can't remember ever meeting anything like this, even at the Far End of the Meadow"—down there in the long grass under the chestnut trees where the stream ran wild and sedgy, and you never knew who or what you might meet. . . .

But the Feeding Legs, the first to cross the stream to the hen-house that morning, was exultant, not disappointed.

"Eleven! My word!" she kept on repeating, and gave the brown hen a succulent breakfast of bread and milk; and gave bread and milk to that absurd wobbling little brood of blacks with the huge heads and webbed feet; then gathered them up into her basket and carried them triumphantly in to the Legs. And shortly afterwards the Owner Legs rushed to the telephone: "We simply must tell you, Sybil! . . . Darling, what do you think? Eleven little black ducklings! . . . We gave her a dozen eggs, I suppose she must have sat on one—No, shouts from the kitchen to say there were only eleven to start with; it's a sheer miracle; you've never seen anything so beautiful! . . . This was a very special clutch we had sent . . . Chinese Game, I think

4

they call them. But we never expected the whole eleven. It remains to be seen," laughed the Owner Legs, accepting congratulations, "it remains to be seen which will be ducks and which drakes . . . No, we shan't be able to tell for ages yet, of course; I was only joking. Come over and see them, won't you? . . . Yes, at once . . . How's Holly? . . . Gone out? My dear, isn't it rather soon to leave them alone? . . . Only just gone out? Well, fetch her back then; I don't believe in these casual mothers."

The brown hen tried to bear with patience the intolerable boasting from her sister with the red-gold feathers, a mother of recognisable chickens who, apart from the yellow of their feathers had beaks which were pointed, not flat, and feet properly divided into claws, not spoked like little umbrellas. "We didn't expect our family to be true blondes like mine," said the arrogant Nordic hen, taking her blonde race for a walk. "But all the same——"

The brown hen was too bewildered herself to summon up much of a defence: "they may go yellow in time, she protested weakly, not believing it herself. "Gander told me that he was grey once when he was quite a little thing, and look at him now. Dazzling!"

But her sister shook her head in pity.

"Quite different. His father was white as snow, as well as his mother. But once a dark strain gets into the blood—ah, well! I mean, you can tell by the texture of their feathers. Never mind; you've let your heart rule your head, that's all, and Gander always said you hadn't even the brains of a Legs!"

Yet whatever her brains, the brown hen had a thoroughly nice nature, and watched over her eleven little grotesques with all the care and tenderness she would have given a fairer, more accountable brood; scolding them when they strayed—and small as they were, they always seemed to be straying; it was lucky the Meadow world was so vast that you could hardly tell, unless you ranged immense distances, that to reach further meadows you would have to cross the dangerous waters of the stream, which no hen could do except at one place, through the Gate of the Feeding Legs and over the plank bridge to the terrace of the Cottage; and of course her little ones were much too young for such an enterprising journey.

A fortnight later she had a further trial to bear: another, an elder sister parading her chickens, yellow, fluffy and correct. Unlike the hen with the red-gold feathers, this white hen took up an attitude of conspicuous gentleness towards the farcical tragedy of her little alien nephews and nieces. It was hard to bear when she pointed out in consolation that she thought that perhaps this morning their heads were slightly rounder than yesterday ... which was so manifestly untrue that those standing near sniggered, and the brown hen burst into tears.

"Come, come," said her elder sister, clucking to

her own impeccable chickens that they should gather round and make an affectionate fuss of their poor weeping aunt. "Come, come, come, come, come. You mustn't give way, for the sake of your—er—your—er—little ones. "Why," brightly, "they're growing so big, you'd hardly know them."

And it was a fact that the ducklings, only a fortnight old, were a family of whom you could be proud, if you did not happen to be a hen.

"Do you know who they remind me of, a little?" said her sister, even more brightly, "in shape, I mean?"

"No, I don't," replied the brown hen in a great hurry. And then she added, with a touch of hysteria: "I don't care *what* you all say; I never went *near* the Sheldrake!"

Two

"HE'S A GOOD HUSBAND," ALL THE MEADOW remarked, full of admiration for Gander; and with a little
envy too, for which of them could ever stretch fancy
into calling Rooster a good husband? "Oh, Goose is
lucky; and she knows it. Look at him now."

Lonely and proud, the Gander stood sentinel, day
after day and night after night, while his mate sat on
her eggs. He would allow no one except the Feeding
Legs to come near her; and they were all afraid of his
fierceness while they respected his preoccupation.
Once a day she felt the need of a little variety and
exercise; so he met her punctiliously at the door of the
hen-house when she came out, flew with her (not too
high, because you never know) the length of the
Meadow and a little beyond, then back again with a
strong beat of wings, both sliding down to the grass
just beside the bucket kept full of fresh water near the

Gate of the Feeding Legs. Again he stood on guard while she made a refreshing toilet, sluicing deep into the water and then flinging back her head with a shower of sparkling drops. After she had done this several times, the Gander escorted her back to the hen-house, and once more stood at his post outside, alert, militant, waiting for news. Nothing would tempt him away from his wife's bedroom—"though I could do with a stiff whisky and soda," he reflected now and then. "I forget who told me that these periods were just as trying for the husband, and by my fatted liver, so they are!"

When at last they brought him the news that he was the father of a lovely little gaggle of seven, he still kept a stiff upper neck and betrayed none of the emotion he felt:

"The Memsahib—?"

"Yes, yes. Doing well. She asked for you first thing."

"May I see them?" was his next question.

"Well, no, I wouldn't just yet. All in good time, my dear fellow. She's a little highly strung, you know. Anyhow, hearty congratulations and all that."

"Thanks. Thanks very much. It's been a strain. I won't deny it has been a strain. And now if I'm not wanted, I'll toddle along to the Club." He enquired with a touch of careless contempt: "I expect the Legs are pleased?"

"I believe you! Pleased isn't the word. You can

hear them honking a mile off. Dunno what's in the air, but I've never known 'em so keen as they are this summer on keeping up the birth-rate. One would think their lives depended on it."

This was a summer of unusual fecundity. The Cottage and the Garden and the Meadow seemed bent on producing more and more life, a heightened importance beyond mere interest and pleasure. The Legs hinted at it in brief, portentous phrases such as: "Winter Crisis," "Food Shortage," "National Emergency," "Cuts in Imports," "Dependent on Home Produce," "Self-Supporting," as though birth in its most innocent and ridiculous farmyard manifestation, had a looming speculative quality; some overhanging fate, dependent on, for instance, a small quirk of feather which might or might not appear, upcurving from the ducklings" tails; dependent on a bunch of tail feathers or a slightly more protuberant crest on the chickens. The Feeding Legs was always making shrewd comment on these terrific points.

So that the birth of Teazle's kittens at about the same time as the second lot of real chickens was a funny sort of relief from strain. Cats and kittens were simply fun, serving no sinister purpose in the distant future. The Legs were growing far too fond of the ducklings, though gradually losing affection for the chickens. As for the goslings, they never left the

Meadow, and unless you were escorted by the Feeding Legs you might not go near them; the other Legs watched respectfully from a distance where, led by parent Goose and Gander, they filed—"like a posse of small grey police," remarked the Nitwit Legs.

"I've never seen police grow gradually whiter"; the Sardonic Legs sometimes showed too clearly that the Nitwit Legs had apparently taken up her residence on his nerves; though in reality he was fond of her, and each understood the other's idiom without acquiring it.

Hastily backing away from the point at issue, she began to chatter ecstatically of the new kittens:

"Two boys and a girl. That's just right, isn't it?"

"What d'you mean by 'just right?'"

The Owner Legs came to the rescue:

"She means that Teazle has always had nearly all girls so far, and we wanted to keep a boy this time, though the trouble is that the girl, the little grey one, is the prettiest."

Immediately a violent discussion sprang up: Gracie had a blue-eyed, half-Persian, seductive charm in her little three-cornered face, enough to make you cry if you were responsive to that easy form of art; but a strong contingent of Legs were in favour of the kitten whom they called Glamour Boy (or alternatively, Juvenile Lead), a handsome lad, also semi-Persian, with long dark fur that had a ruddy sheen over it, and a tail which one day would be long and plumy;

a smashing tail. And then there was Tiger Tim. The Nitwit Legs pressed his claims as being the least obvious. One would say that Tiger Tim had never even smelt a Persian. Nor had he the lithe limber movements of Holly, his half-cousin once removed, with a distant Siamese strain in her ancestry. He was timid and did not sport around with his brother and sister; if he could not be curled up close beside Teazle, pathetically searching for her portable dairy, he preferred to slip away by himself and lie concealed under the raised porch of the summerhouse. Already he showed in miniature the beautiful striped markings of his jungle prototype.

"It really gives one a queer little thrill to see him moving about in the undergrowth of the herbaceous border," said the Owner Legs; "not that our herbaceous border ought to have an undergrowth. I wish one of you *liked* gardening." Silence.

Then the Nitwit Legs began again:

"*Can't* we keep Tiger Tim? Teazle likes him best."

And that was perfectly true. Teazle did. A cat of poise and character, though cold and perverse, she drove her two handsomer kittens from her side, telling them she was sick and tired of motherhood and they must go and fend for themselves; but for Tiger Tim, thin and frightened, with his faintly hobgoblin appeal, she showed genuine kindness and an anxiety that he should not be docked of his elevenses, however inconvenient to herself.

"Eyewash," said the Sardonic Legs. "Now she has her figure back, all she cares for is—" He described in Restoration terms what Teazle cared for.

"Poor little beast!"

"Why? Are you going to—?"

The Owner Legs nodded, and a loud wail rose from the Nitwit Legs:

"Oh, you can't. You can't possibly. Not Teazle!"

"Fraid we have to. She never stops. Kittens about every six weeks." (This was an exaggeration.) "And the garden at night is like a hunting-field in full cry. If we'd had her doctored to begin with—but she was already a year old when she came, and it's dangerous by then. This young man," she indicated Tony the Glamour Boy, "can go to the vet in a couple of months, and they can put Teazle away painlessly at the same time."

"At least you ought try to find a home for her."

"Don't be an ass! I've ransacked five counties for a home for Teazle. 'Isn't he a pretty cat?' everybody says admiringly. Then I explain."

"Well, what about Gracie? Are you going to have her executed as well?"

The Sardonic Legs groaned. "Executed! That's right; work it up into melodrama!"

Holly's Legs had joined them, interrupting the discussion while she did an ecstasy over the kittens. Directly she subsided, the Nitwit Legs appealed to her as a sure ally against the cruel disposal of Teazle simply because Teazle let rip her natural instincts so prettily on moonlit (and other) nights.

But she did not get the indignant backing for which she had confidently hoped. After an embarrassed silence and one or two false starts, Holly's Legs confessed what was in her mind . . .

The Nitwit Legs gave her one shuddering look— "Et tu, Brute"—and turned away, picked up Tiger and cuddled him, spoke loving words to Teazle, praised Gracie's agility and Glamour Boy's already admirable whiskers.

"Quite right," said the Sardonic Legs, commending Holly's Legs heartily for her good sense and lack of sentimentality, and hiding his surprise, for she *was* usually sentimental over animals.

"I hate doing it. I don't know how I'm going to bear it when the time comes. But really, I can hardly get her home to feed her kittens, and they're barely a fortnight old. And I can't bear having to drown kittens—I can't *bear* it. And if in future I have to cope with nine at a time —for all I know it may be seventeen in her next litter. And I've had to drown so many, because you know one can't find homes for the girls however much one tries to wrap it up that they *are* girls."

(". . .Your mind, dear heart, is like a cess-pit," said the Owner Legs to the Sardonic Legs, after his aside.)

"—And I don't see how any of us can manage to feed more than one cat with the sort of winter we're

14

going to have, our rations down to nothing and prices going up by leaps and bounds."

"They say the nation will be half-starved unless we all do our share."

"Yes—well—keeping a cat who keeps on having kittens over and over and over again would hardly count as doing one's share, I'm afraid. It isn't that I grudge Holly anything—"

"I should," said the Sardonic Legs. "I'd grudge her everything. Beautiful but beastly."

"I can't deny it; she is unloving except—oh, well—*except*, you know. Of course, I won't have her put to sleep until I've found good homes for all the *male* little silver angels and chosen the one I'm going to keep myself. Though I think I've spotted him already." Her face beamed with the love that Holly might have claimed, but had flung away for more wanton passions.

"And I imagine when she goes—" the Sardonic Legs disregarded the euphemism "put to sleep"—"all the little *female* silvery angels will have to go with her?"

The Nitwit Legs made choking sounds, so the Owner Legs was glad of a diversion swishing up the stream; or rather, of three diversions:

"There's Donald, Dilly, and Dally. We don't see much of them lately except at meal times. Of course they're no relation of the new ones, so I suppose they resent them."

"Not any of them? Have I got it wrong? I thought one of them was the mother?"

For Donald, Dilly, and Dally had been named before the determination of their sex; but all three of them, white, grey and brown, proved after all to be ducks.

"No, they won't sit, so we had to put the eggs under a hen; ducks are notoriously bad sitters; these are just aunts by courtesy and not much of that on either side. They've only met at feeding-time."

"Not on the stream?"

"The ducklings haven't been launched yet. Donald, Dilly, and Dally still own the stream, especially Donald." And the Owner Legs added carelessly, forgetting what had been a delicate subject of debate, "They've been excellent layers, but they're getting very old" (the Sardonic Legs grinned), "so they're for it as soon as—"

Her reflections were broken by loud accusing wails from the Nitwit Legs, for whom the future at the Cottage was rapidly taking on the aspect of a prolonged massacre:

"You can't eat Donald, Dilly, and Dally! You can't possibly! You told me you'd had them for years—"

"Quite," said the Sardonic Legs. "Only we're not talking of old and faithful servants; one would hardly send those to the pot, but luckily one can when it's ducks."

"Oh, well, it won't be for some time yet," said the Owner Legs hastily, wondering why it was that in all conversations the prevailing dangerous theme would persistently recur however hard you tried to avoid it.

"How old are they?" asked Holly's Legs.

"A good four years, I think; let me see—would they be four or five? I know they were hatched out in the winter, because one night after we'd scooped in the other two we couldn't find Donald anywhere, and shut them up, and it was pitch black, and then we heard faint quacks in the thick tangle of bushes between the hen-house and the stream. It was terribly difficult to stalk her down, but we could just have done it by her infant quacks if the bell-ringers hadn't suddenly started pealing and clanging just over there in the Church tower. It was their Practice Hour. So we had to give up, and little Donald had her first night out."

"Couldn't you have asked them to stop for a few minutes?" asked the Nitwit Legs, who loved animal anecdotes.

"No, dear. We couldn't."

"Why not?"

"Because it would have sounded silly: 'Please stop, we're looking for a duckling in the bushes in the dark.'"

"I've heard you all say much sillier things than that," said the Nitwit Legs, unexpectedly showing spirit. "I'd have asked if I'd been here."

"We know you would."

"Look!" exclaimed Holly's Legs suddenly, pointing.

A single file of greyish-black ducklings, looking absurdly small and enterprising, and unattended by mother, governess, or nurse, was waddling along the grass on the opposite side of the stream till it stopped at a dip in the bank between the willows, nearly opposite to where the Legs were congregated on the lawn. Then, as though they had discussed the whole matter between themselves, each truant one by one did a sort of downward scramble and a slither and a plop into the water.

Once in, being ducklings, they swam.

"They know what streams are for," murmured the Sardonic Legs. "No call for anxiety."

The Nitwit Legs made ecstatic noises, and for once the others did not squash her; they felt a little the same themselves.

All were in but one, when— "Lo!" exclaimed the Owner Legs, lifting her eyes; "who comes here?"

Tearing along after the ducklings was their agitated foster-mother, the brown hen.

"'Can a mother's tender care,'" quoted the Sardonic Legs, "'fail towards the brood she bear?' Now what's she going to do?"

They all watched with breathless interest. The hen stood as near as she dared to the brink, clucking and scolding.

"'Come back, come back, she cried in grief, across the stormy water. . . .'"

"Oh, do shut up! She doesn't understand that they can swim! Can't someone tell her it's all right?"

The black ducklings took not the slightest notice of the clucks. They were having the time of their lives, and for the first time in their lives. But the brown hen

obviously believed they were drowning. Was there no one else to go to the rescue? No one who cared? Summoning her courage, shutting her eyes, and bracing every nerve as she bade farewell to earth and grass and Meadow beneath her feet, she flapped in.

With a short, sharp oath the Sardonic Legs strode in and caught her as she swirled by. The water was about two feet deep, flowing clear and pellucid towards the tributary flowing towards the Thames which flowed towards the sea. But beneath the bright green cresses and water-weeds, the mud reached to well above his knees, and it was quite difficult to drag himself up and out while carrying a dripping struggling hen.

("Let me go! Let me go! Let me drown with my children!")

"There, you simple, addle-pated, egg-bound old fool." He set her down gently on the lawn.

"That's no good; she'll only go in again. Better take her along to the kitchen and let them dry her. Would you ever have guessed that even a hen would show so little sense?"

"Or so much love?" suggested the Nitwit Legs in tones of tenderest reproach.

Three

"I KNOW HE'S MY NEPHEW. MORE'S THE pity; the
only survivor of my poor dear sister's last gaggle before
she . . ." Gander subsided into that brooding silence
which overcame all the Meadow residents whenever
the natural flow of talk happened to lead round to a
sudden vanishing. It was an understood thing among
them that this silence had to be respected and the
sentence allowed to lapse without questions. Panic had
something to do with it, and delicacy; most of all,
perhaps, tradition. The Meadow was a free republic
where they could all do more or less as they pleased, of
course within reason—except when from the Cottage
side of the stream, the Stable Legs and the Feeding
Legs swooped over without their usual benevolent
intentions. It did not happen often; one could trust the
Legs, rely on them, follow them in an indistinguishable
orchestra of clacking, gabbling, gobbling, interest over
what they might be carrying in bucket, basket, or

saucepan. One could even despise the Legs for the silly lives they led and for their jumping to silly conclusions about the Meadow folk about whom really they knew so little.

But every now and then . . . one did not despise the Legs.

The Literary Gander, the same Gander who was causing so much trouble to his military-minded Uncle in the Meadow, sometimes referred to them as Clotho, Lachesis, and Atropos; he had been on the Classical side at his College until the sudden death of his parents and aunt (about Christmas time). When it was found they had left no money, their son had to return home to take up his farm duties—which, being what he was, he failed to do.

Gander remarked: "I wish he wouldn't come over from opposite so often. You shouldn't encourage him, my dear. Let him," a trifle ambiguously, "stew in his own juice."

The Gentle Goose who owned him for her lord, and two months before had borne him such a handsome healthy file of offspring, murmured a few words to soothe him; such as that she was sure he was really fond of his nephew and proud of his abilities; and after all he had no mother, nor father either, so it was nice for him to step over and see his young cousins who were all very fond of him.

"That's just it," snapped Gander. "He's a bad influence. D'you know I've actually heard the feller reciting *poetry* to them?"

"Tsss, tss, tss," the Goose hissed in soft deprecation and with a touch of alarm.

"Poetry!" snorted the outraged uncle. "And all his notions are wrong; don't know where he picked 'em up; my own kith and kin full of pacifist nonsense! — You'd hardly believe it, but I caught him out teaching his cousins not to do the goose-step; said it had been at the root of some trumpery war that the Legs played at a few hundred years ago . . . I don't know . . . no business of ours anyhow. Tried to teach 'em some disgusting sort of pansy sway instead of putting out first one leg and then the other, straight and stiff as I'm training them to do. Sway, indeed! No one's ever swayed in our family before. But don't worry, my dear, he didn't succeed. Look at them now." He watched with approval the line of young geese, still in their adolescent gray feathers, stepping smartly towards them through the long grass. "Told them to be back from their walk sharp when the sun lay over the top of the third walnut-tree, and here they are, good as gold, coming for their bed-time story. Not a straggler among 'em; I've no patience with stragglers."

He was very much of a family Gander, for all his sharp autocratic ways, and liked to see them standing round him in their own portion of the Meadow, between the pump and the hedge, whilst, as an alternative influence to that infernal young meddler from over the road, he rewarded their obedience with the true story of how the Leg army at Agincourt owed their victory entirely to the grey geese who had supplied quills for the arrows of the Archer Legs; who sped them straight and true among the mounted Legs of the French Army, and completely routed them.

"I'll say this for the Legs; they were grateful, and so they should have been. Ever since then, our tribe have been awarded right-of-way over all pedestrian Legs and all motoring Legs, and if any legal dispute arises—" he brought forth the climax with pride, "—judgement is given for the geese. There are certain dangers, my dear goslings, against which you must always be prepared and on guard, but any of us can always cross from one side of the road to another with immunity."

At that precise moment, having keen eyesight, he descried his unwelcome nephew crossing the road with immunity from the Farm Opposite, and heartily wished some motorist might come along who had not heard of the privilege that dated from the victory of Agincourt. Hoping to distract his listeners, he rapidly passed to another story, rather to their surprise, because one per evening had been their usual allowance. The Gander found it difficult, however, to do himself justice as a raconteur in his further patriotic story of the Geese who saved the Capitol by cackling loudly to announce the stealthy approach of Rome's enemies, and how the Romans made public provision for them as a reward for their vigilance. His nephew, on the outskirts of the group, listened with insufferable patronage: "Yes, dear Uncle, and what comes next?"—enough to drive any self-respecting Gander to the bucket. However, he just managed to finish his tale, and then the gaggle became aware of their cousin and hailed him with delight, asking him innocently if he had ever heard these enthralling legends? and was he not proud to be a gander, since without them the Legs, whether English or Roman, would certainly never have overcome their dastardly foes?

"I'm a bit surprised your Pater includes a lot of damn Wop geese with ours," remarked the wicked young Gander, "but don't mind me, Uncle; go on; I'm enjoying it."

"There isn't anything to go on about," severely. "Isn't it somewhat late for you to be out? When you're as old as I am—"

"Oh, I never will be; I'm not that type. Those whom the gods love, you know, die young."

But it was here that the Military Gander at last scored a point in rather a big way: "You've got it wrong," he snapped. "Comes of too much book-learning. Those whom the *Legs* love—" He stopped. The sinister implication hung in the air. The Literary Gander turned and strolled away with that pansy sway which had become inalienable to his nature—and almost fell over the eleven ducklings who happened to be lying in the grass round the gate. With his genuine tenderness for the very young, their credulity, their innocence, their dewiness, their impressionable minds, he stayed with them and helped to restore his prestige in his own sight by the recitation of a piece of poetry suitable to their weeks and beaks:

> "Four ducks on a pond,
> A grass-bank beyond,
> A blue sky of spring,
> White clouds on the wing;
> What a little thing
> > To remember for years—
> > To remember with tears!"

It was only a short poem, so he was surprised and a little aggrieved, at the end of it, to find that the audience whom he had believed hanging upon his words, had melted away; for like all born reciters, he kept his eyes a little raised and fixed on the middle distance.

... No, one had remained. One small black attentive duckling, too interested to be timid with this fine-looking well-set-up stranger from over the road, whom he knew by sight and had long admired. "Please, why did he—the Legs—remember them with tears? What was there to cry about? Because there were only four of them on the pond? What is a pond? There are eleven of us; would that make Legs cry more or not cry at all?"

The Literary Gander smiled indulgently: a good little thing, a bright little thing, a respectful little thing;

very low on the ground, but nevertheless appreciative of the privilege of listening to him; such perspicacity should have its reward:

"Never mind why Legs cry. Life's too short for us to bother about whether they're crying or laughing. Eleven? Thats a fine brood; your Pater and Mater must be pleased." He always referred to parents by their Roman form of address, "just to be different" (according to his Uncle, who forbade it from his own gaggle).

Naturally, what with one thing and another, the Duckling knew nothing of either paters or maters: "Will you please tell me some more poetry? I liked the piece about the ducks, but I'd like to hear something about *your* family, please."

The Literary Gander, thus encouraged, became a Solitary Gander of Noble Ancestry. Unluckily, when thus given his head he forgot everything he had heard or made up about his Noble Ancestors except for a few vague romantic bits about a Snow Goose whom the Legs honoured for its fearless behaviour at a placed called Dunkirk. Searching his memory, for it was a pity to have the theatre full and attentive and then fluff his lines, he actually lowered himself to repeat his Uncle's two stories with the stress removed from the military to the poetic aspect; afterwards remarking carelessly that the modern stuff was more interesting, and that one outgrew poetry for prose:

"There was a famous book about us by a Legs called Galsworthy—no, I'm mistaken; that was all about a Swan Song; I must have been thinking of the French Legs called Proust. No, his was about a Swann too . . ."

"Swan?" repeated the Duckling fascinated, "what is a swan? Are there any in the Meadow?"

The Literary Gander shook his head. He was not too clear himself about swans, having heard only rumours here and there. "There was one very famous Swan-Legs called Pavlova; dead now; she was *always* dying. And one other, a princess with eleven brothers—"

"Eleven . . ." breathed the Duckling.

"Yes, and they all flew away without their shirts on—No, with their shirts on—No, without—No, let me see," he racked his brains for the story of the Flying Swans. "The Princess threw their shirts over them when they were flying past her window, and so they were turned back into Legs except one; she hadn't finished his shirt, and thus he always remained different with a bit of him not Leg-like. He was the youngest prince and her favourite brother." A few more items of the tale came drifting back like feathers that have been shed. "They had been put under a spell, you see."

The Duckling did not want to keep on asking too many questions; he supposed a shirt and a spell were the same thing: "I've heard the Feeding Legs say that the Stable Legs puts on a clean spell every day." He was anxious not to seem stupid, now that he had found this wonderful new patron, but he could not quite get this story clear, except that they had or had not worn shirts, and that one of the eleven (that was the part he liked best) was different from the rest.

"Is a swan song very beautiful? Have you ever heard it?"

"More questions! Never mind; it shows your mind is alive and not always on the ground. We must see a lot of each other, you and I." He found the Duckling's company more congenial than that of all his cousins put together, though he had not quite realized that it was because Duckling thought him more wonderful than all his cousins put together. So again he took up his stand for recitation:

"The silver swan who living had no note
As death approached, unlocked her silent throat.
Leaning her breast against—against—against the kitchen door,
Thus sang her first and last, and sang no more—"

but Gander deliberately stopped here, leaving out the last two lines for he had always deemed them unworthy of the rest:

("Farewell all joys. 0 death, come close mine eyes.
More geese than swans now live, more fools than wise.")

Duckling was enchanted by the melancholy idea of a song that every swan sang only once in a lifetime, just before its end; and wished he could people the whole of the wild end of the Meadow with dying swans lifting their voices in farewell.

"Do they live to be very old?"

"Sometimes, yes."

"Do they never sing before they die?"

"No, never."

"Who told them they mustn't?"

"Instinct, and sorrowful intuition."

"Oh"—a long pause.

Then Gander said slowly: "There has been one swan—the Swan of swans—a Royal Swan—the Swan of Avon—who could keep on singing all his life."

"And not die?"

"No, he never died."

"Never?"

"Never, little Duckling. The Swan of Avon has never died."

"What's Avon?"

"A corruption of heaven," replied the Gander . . . though not at once, for he had to search in the Oxford part of his mind, a little rusty from disuse.

"And what's heaven?"

The Literary Gander might have replied, "The Happy Meadows," but he was not at all sure he believed in them; anyhow, Sunday School teaching was hardly in his line, so he fell back on the usual refuge of the much too clever:

"You'd better ask your mother."

"Oh, she won't know. She doesn't know anything." Duckling conformed to popular opinion in
this; the eleven had very little respect for their hen-
brained foster-parent.

"What are swans like when they're born?" he
demanded suddenly. "As beautiful as when they grow
up?"

"On the contrary, exceptionally ugly" . . . the
Gander burst out laughing, as though suddenly re-
minded of a good tale —"By a Danish-Legs. Listen:

Once upon a time . . ." Duckling felt more at home now; once-upon-a-time was a phrase he had heard before, though never with such promise.

"Once upon a time, a mother duck sat day after day on her nest without moving, till at last she had a family of ducklings, all pretty and fluffy and downy, and they cheeped and chirped and ran about, and she was very proud of them. All except one. One of the ducklings wasn't small and pretty like the rest of them; it was awkward and clumsy and never seemed to know what to do with itself, so its brethren mocked it, and the mother duck scolded it, and at last it went away because it was so miserable, and hid itself in a field at the other end of the world, and cried because it was such an ugly colour, and thought it could only be happy if it was exactly like the other ducklings, for now nobody could ever love it and it might as well be dead."

His listener was breathless; he could barely find voice enough to ask, through choking sobs: "Yes . . . and what happened then?"

The Literary Gander was faced with a hiatus; a hiatus is a very grave thing in the mind of a performer; and not only a hiatus, but an attack of amnesia, so between hiatus and amnesia he simply did not know how to answer Duckling's request to know what happened then. All he could remember from the fairy-story was its end: "The Ugly Duckling turned out to be a beautiful white swan, admired by all who saw him, and went to live with the other swans and was the most beautiful of them all, and quite forgot that he had ever been an Ugly Duckling."

A cheeky young cockerel, unperceived by either, broke into their little circle of enchantment. He came quite close, terribly pleased with his wit and aptness, and cried to the Literary Gander loudly and fearlessly, with a familiarity unbecoming to his age:

"Goosey Goosey Gander,
 Whither do you wander?
Upstairs and downstairs
And in my lady's chamber.
There I met an old man
Who wouldn't say his prayers—"

—But he was interrupted by a sequence of events so swift that the Literary Gander and the Duckling were hardly aware of what had happened before it was all over.

. . . "Yes, that one over there; he's just about ready," said the Feeding Legs.

The Stable Legs strode over to the little group, and scattered some corn. The greedy young cockerel pecked at it; he got seized by one leg—a quick wrench of a vertebra in his neck—and then he was carried along, limp and dangling, over the bridge to the shed by the kitchen, and the door slammed.

Duckling asked with bated breath: "Was that done to him because he was being so rude to you?"

"Probably." Gander did not really think so, but curt reality had turned his stomach queasy, too queasy for him to flavour the episode with any brilliant Olympian references to Nemesis and Fate and the Vengeance of the Gods.

Duckling was very young; he noticed that some grains still lay on the ground near by; with pretty manners rare in any of the Meadow residents, he held back for an instant and asked: "Won't you—" Gander shook his head, and with something less than his usual sway, departed for his home across the road. The urchin cockerel had been impudent, but he had desired no revenge. Besides, was it revenge? Did the Legs care for any one of them beyond—beyond what he had seen just now? Apprehension lay heavy on his mind as he passed through the gap in the hedge to his own farm paddock; and poetry had died in him . . . at the moment he had no taste left for those neat quotations that usually ministered to his harmless vanity, or he might have murmured with Randal of the old ballad: "Mother, oh Mother, make my bed soon, For I'm sick to the heart and I fain would lay doon."

He lay doon.

Left alone to gobble or meditate, Duckling found the former process gradually slowing up, while the latter took possession. Presently he was eating in a sort of daze . . . and presently he was not eating at all, though a few tempting grains still lay around him.

None of the Meadow residents had come near to intrude on his thoughts . . . of an Ugly Duckling different from the rest, always apart while they played and gambolled in the stream, dipping their beaks into the weed in search of flies or tadpoles, chasing each other with merry splashings, a romping, carefree crowd of brothers and sisters. But had he not always been different? Ever since that moment on the bank when the others had one by one taken to the water, and he, last of the file, was just going to flop in himself, when their foster-mother came tearing along and hurled herself into the stream to rescue them, and was nearly drowned. Had the Legs not been present . . . Duckling still preferred not to remember the shuddering sight of his mother struggling and sinking, swirled helplessly in the current, bumped against the bank . . . His flotilla of brothers and sisters had been first astonished, and then, assured of the safety of Old Ma Pot-Luck (as they had nicknamed her among themselves) rolled over and under and over again, quacking with heartless merriment, never noticing one of their number still left on the willow bank. Often he had wondered how they could possibly behave as though water were a natural element, kind and not cruel and perilous? Little nervous shivers rippled down his back-feathers whenever he recalled those loud terrified squawks for help. Trust himself to that fatal element? Never! A reluctance too tough and strong to overcome kept him on dry land where he could feel his webbed feet firmly pressing into the hard safe earth. Of course it was not fear. Of course he was not a funk, as they sometimes called him when they summoned him to join them: "You can't think how exciting it is in the cool squelchy weeds among the willow roots!"

But just suppose . . . Suppose the kind and handsome young Gander, his patron and his hero, had let fall a solution to the whole bewildering enigma of his existence? Suppose history were repeating itself? Or suppose even— (supposes swelled and became more fantastic and delightful every moment, and more comforting)—supposing the Danish-Legs had had a pre-natal vision (not his own natal; somebody else's). For it was not likely, was it, that this miraculous story could actually happen twice? "Of me he wrote!" He, an Ugly Duckling, was no duckling at all; and in time they would find out their mistake, and all the Meadow would pay him obeisance, and the Legs would exclaim how wrong they had been, how foolish, how mistaken . . . "Then they'll be sorry" (it always worked out to "then they'll be sorry")—for they would realise at last that he was a swan, a beautiful graceful swan.

A little giddy and dazed by the enormous change in his prospects wrought by this brief but pregnant half-hour, Duckling looked round for the Literary Gander so that he might ask him more and more and more about swans, having already forgotten most of what he had been told. How should he begin to fit himself for his classical destiny? Only one item stuck in his memory; swans flew, swans did not swim . . . Something about white shirts with ruffles at the neck, or were swans altogether white?

He would make it his business to find out. And meanwhile he vowed with a grandeur that would be worse before it was better, that he would endure all obloquy from those buffoons who believed themselves to be his brothers and sisters, now that he was dedicated to the fair certainty of ultimate swanhood.

Four

THE BROWN HEN WAYLAID THE BIG BLACK Rooster
as he was stepping arrogantly through the meadowsweet in the direction of the pump under the
gooseberry-pippin tree, where three or four of his
other wives (those who were not broody) hung about,
afraid to solicit, yet anxious for his lordly favour.

"Well, little one," he said, looking down on her
kindly enough, "still off-colour?" and he glanced
disparagingly at her wattles. "You haven't laid an egg
since I don't know when."

The little brown hen plucked up courage. "You
haven't been round . . . as often as you used to," she
murmured. It was the truth and he knew it. But then
he had never found her particularly stimulating. The
mother type was not attractive. Inevitably they lost
their looks for a short time; when it was to be your
own youngsters, you could put up with it; her sister

38

Rhoda, with the red-gold feathers, for instance; he was mighty proud of her offspring; two of them were black with golden collars. And even then she didn't fuss about them as the little brown hen still fussed round in vain pursuit of her outrageous web-footed foster-children. All very well for her to deny having encountered the Sheldrake; all hens are liars, he decided, and they all fell for a showy vagabond type of no breeding and obscure ancestry. He reflected complacently on his own grandfather, Spur 'O the East, who (in all Poultry Shows) had been awarded the highest of honours.

Bored by their dialogue, he strutted off on some conventional excuse.

The brown hen gazed after him wistfully. How splendid he was, her chanticleer; how debonair, how noble, what a voice! Lucky the wife who could keep his love so that he never strayed from her side. There must be some secret way, the way of a hen with a cock?—

"I wonder," she mused, for her conscience was her trouble, "I wonder if it's *wrong* to hate one's sister?"

Life in the Meadow was full of worries: those ducklings of hers—for Dilly had enlightened her as to their species, though even then the mystery was not quite cleared up—those ducklings were never off the water, now they had found it. Never again did she hurl herself after them (she could have contributed a powerful article to the Meadow World Gazette on "How It Feels After Drowning"—600 words—no pay). Nevertheless, she could not leave well alone, but had to spend a large part of her life standing on the bank, apprehensive for their safety and calling out quite futile suggestions about a nice quiet game of play with the chickabiddies in the Meadow: "And *do* be careful, darlings, how you land. It's so slippery just there."

The Rooster; the ducklings; and here was the third worry, mooching and moping along the bank, as usual solitary. Perhaps a little motherly talk might do some good.

"Well," she started off brightly, "all by yourself?" Duckling shook his shoulders in a petulant fashion. It was not worth replying to that sort of silly question.

"Now listen, darling. I'm not cross with you, you mustn't think that. I love all my ducklings alike. But I do wish you'd behave a little more *like* a duckling"— an odd ambition for the hen.

"Why should I?" muttered Duckling, and (Hassan fashion) he dipped the wings of complacence into the cistern of secret anticipation.

"Because it's nicer, dear, for everyone, when we see you merry and carefree and romping with the others. We're a very cheerful community here in the Meadow, and you must try to be cheerful too and shake off all your foolish little troubles, like—like water off a duck's back. Live up to your family motto; a very good motto, I always think. Repeat it now."

There was a gleam of mischief in Duckling's eyes

as he tendered the motto in its original French:

"Je ne tiens pas l'eau
  Sur le dos."

"Oh *dear*!" cried the Brown Hen in fresh anxiety, "I *do* hope you're not going to be clever. I'd even rather you went swimming."

"Have you ever noticed," said the Owner Legs "that one duckling never goes in the water with the rest?"

The Sardonic Legs *had* noticed, but had been afraid to mention it for fear of what idiocies it might release from the Nitwit Legs, who till now had oddly enough overlooked this promising opening for pathetic speculation:

"Oh, *poor* little mite! Perhaps the others are unkind to it! They're terribly rough the way they duck each other—"

But this was too much for her companions, who went off into shouts of laughter.

"No wonder your protégé is afraid to join in the ragging."

The Nitwit Legs rightly pointed out that it was a bit illogical to refer to "her" protégé when it was they, not she, who had called attention to its aloof habits.

"But do you think it's ill? Ought we to ring up the vet, or is a vet only for foot-and-mouth disease and things like that?"

"I don't think your duckling has foot-and-mouth disease. It looks just the same as the rest of the flotilla; appetite all right, and rushes about all over the Meadow. I should say it's just got some idea in it's head about not getting its feet wet." The Sardonic Legs indicated where a solitary duckling was stepping across the plank bridge from the Meadow to the miniature brick terrace outside the sitting-room. Arrived at its destination, it turned and very deliberately walked back again, ignoring its brethren who were filing up to the bank from the Meadow, and with an occasional side-slip slithering into the stream. After one proud look, the reverse of convivial, the Duckling mooched off, turning in its toes and wobbling its bottom.

"How sad to be an Only Child without Kith or Kin. Often when I hear the shouts of those other happy ducklings playing with their brothers and sisters in the next-door garden, riding their ponies round the paddock, pummelling each other as they race off to rob the orchard—"

The Nitwit Legs stopped his parody with a reproachful, "It's all very well, but I'm an only child myself, and it is lonely, and I know just how it feels."

"You've missed the whole point, my girl; the symptoms of an only child are not for a duckling with ten brothers and sisters all exactly the same age. But it's easy to see that that little black piece of affectation has already become your own precious white-headed boy! I expect when you were a little wistful curly-headed mite, you read *Misunderstood* and *Hoodie* and *Dombey and Son* and *Sara Crewe*; a whole nursery bookshelf about the smallest and the ugliest and the saddest of the family who when they died turned out to be the brightest, bravest, lovingest, beautifullest—"

The Nitwit Legs, who remembered her nursery bookshelf better than the Owner Legs, scored here by putting her right on several points:

"Little Humphrey from *Misunderstood* had always been by nature bold and brave and strong and beautiful. It was his younger brother, little Miles, fair and sickly and wistful, who was nearly drowned, and rescued by Humphrey who died of pneumonia afterwards with everybody standing round being sorry they'd been so wrong about him." The Owner Legs admitted to an inaccuracy. "But I swear I'm right over little Hoodie; she was fundamentally an Apartist."

"I suppose so. I wrote a piece of poetry about her when I was only ten; I called it, 'Nobody Loves Me.'"

The Owner Legs interrupted in a great hurry, for she was afraid they might have to hear "Nobody Loves Me" from beginning to end. "As a matter of fact, your duckling isn't really the smallest or the ugliest of the batch, nor on the other hand the most radiant and beautiful. I should say he's about four from the top when you can sort them out."

The Nitwit Legs ploughed on: "Little Paul died, but he wasn't misunderstood or left out or not wanted; because he was his father's favourite, and his sister

Florence's—he called her Floy—and his Aunt Louisa Chick loved him and so did Susan Nipper and Mr. Toots, and—and—oh yes, of course Polly his first nurse—"

"Spare us. It's quite clear that your protégé isn't Little Paul and isn't Little Humphrey or Little Arthur or Little Hoodie or Little Lord Fauntleroy or—"

"Little-All-Alone?" suggested the Nitwit Legs, trying to hit on the perfect name for the duckling of her adoption.

The Sardonic Legs made his first and last contribution: "Little Stuff-and-Nonsense."

And this was the name that stuck.

Five

DUCKLING'S STATE OF MIND AFTER HIS strange interesting half-hour with the Literary Gander from over the road, was that of needing constant reassurance, or elation would sink to doubt, and doubt to despondency. How unlucky that his Gander lived so far away, and not in the Meadow World which was full of stupid creatures who never talked about swans or swan-songs or anything really vital; merely a lot of senseless gabbling and gobbling about how the quality of their meals had gone down, and how the Feeding Legs seemed to think she could chuck in anything—old apple-parings and bad carrots and potato-peel and cabbage stalks and rotten tomatoes and trouser-buttons, just to make it look more. Duckling lusted for further intelligence on the romantic ways and habits of the swan he was to become; all other topics had become unbearably dull. Actually he had the nerve to go up to the Military Gander and ask him if (while on sentry duty perhaps) he had ever watched a flight of swans over the treetops? Gander had hissed for fully twenty minutes afterwards, his neck stretched out perfectly straight, so that even the Feeding Legs feared to come near him and wondered if he were sickening for something.

It was such a boring existence, waddling to and fro among the fragrant meadowsweet; drawing near to the gossiping groups beside the pump in the vain hope that they *might* be talking about swans. They never were, of course. From morn till night a continual frustration, yet still the dream was there. How long before it could be realised? Had the Literary Gander made any mention of the time that must pass between the persecution of an Ugly Duckling and the glorious transformation scene?

Made even more restless on a certain hot July noon by the sight of his ten brethren wallowing in the coolness of the stream, sending a shower and scatter of glittering drops as they splashed at their endless infantile games, he suddenly determined that he could no longer feel envious and look contemptuous through eternities of summer weather; he had to have, so to speak, something more to go on. Let them sport in trailing weed and muddy water; he turned his back upon his birthright; for had not the lordly Gander affirmed that he had a right to a more magnificent destiny? So he sneaked under the arch and up the little incline from the stream to the road on the further side of the group of cottages; then, dodging the traffic, over the road past the small triangular green with the three great chestnut trees, into the deep overgrown ditch full of nettles and slime, and eventually, frightened at his own temerity, through the slats of the fence that guarded the paddock of the Farm Opposite. It was the first time he had ever roamed so far alone, and his heart beat fast under his wing feathers, and his little crop felt as though it would burst with emotion. Wildly he looked around at great horned beasts lumbering and munching without direction or purpose; but yonder, under the shade of an up-ended blue farm cart, he suddenly spied a curve of brilliant white; and regarding the Gander as sanctuary in an unfamiliar world, ran towards him in a sort of scramble and lurch, remembering nevertheless to restrain an odd compulsion to draw his attention by loud quacking noises, for swans, even embryo swans, could never quack; they sang once and then died, and he did not wish to die in swan-song before he *was* a swan. In a confused sort of way he told himself it was only auto-hysteria; a desire to copy Donald, Dilly, and Dally.

The Literary Gander was always ready to be kind to his little disciple; though naturally puzzled at the perpetual volley of questions regarding a certain mysterious scintillating creature of the air which had seemingly clutched the Duckling's fancy. He could not even recall clearly what he had told him that evening when they had both been at least a fortnight younger than now. He had not been across lately to see his Uncle, though the old fellow missed him, and it was fun to tease him by teaching his cousins not to goose-step. Something had happened last time he was there, he had forgotten exactly what, which had made the Meadow in retrospect a little formidable, even a little eerie . . . In a good-natured attempt to satisfy the little thing, he told him (not too lucidly) the plot of a play by a Norway-Legs called "The Wild Duck"— ("We are not amused," was the politely unspoken verdict). And then repeated some more poetry about a Swan who seemed to have been perpetually couchant while regardant of a certain Leda-Legs . . . Which still, how-ever, was not quite what Duckling wanted, for it did not even begin to tell him how *soon* he might expect to show those first faint but unmistakable signs of metamorphosis which would mark him out as wholly and romantically different from his brethren. It would be some help, or at least it would strengthen his faith in what was to happen, if only they would start calling him ugly, but as yet they hardly seemed to have no-ticed it; only that he would not swim. None of this could be clearly explained to the Literary Gander; it was all too vague and tumbled; presumptuous too, perhaps. Besides, though still in the nursery of his days, wisdom stealing in from beyond warned him that if you tell your dreams, they never hatch out; they should be caressed in the dark.

The Literary Gander was indeed beginning to be a little bothered by Duckling's persistence, especially since, as far as he could see, it appeared to lead nowhere. "Is Great-great-grandma Hen still alive, over in the Meadow?" he enquired. "I don't suppose she gets out much. They say she's over 3,000 days old, and has nearly lost her wits. Come to think of it, I caught a glimpse of her not long ago behind your Hen-House, with pallid wattles and red eyes, her dirty fawn feathers ballooning round her and dropping every time she moved. Well, you never can tell; she says she was a beauty in her youth, and there's nobody left to contradict her."

"What did she do, to grow so old as all that?" asked Duckling, awestruck.

"Oh, I expect she was pretty spry and cunning in middle age and so escaped boi—escaped until it was no good any more." Gander always checked when it came to actual mention of what happened to middle-aged hens and old hens but not to very very very old hens like Grandma. "So they let her live," he finished. "She originally came from some great place beyond the Meadow, and may actually have seen a swan."

"Seen a swan!" Duckling was barely able to articulate, the idea seemed so heavenly and improbable.

"She may. They're not fabulous creatures, you know, like unicorns and dragons. No," hastily, "don't ask me to explain about them; it's too late and would take too long. Besides," with a touch of offence, "Leda was swan-struck, but you hardly listened—No, it's all right, don't apologise, I'm not cross; you're a foolish little thing but you'll learn; and at any rate you don't belong to the set that play games. Now you run along to Grandma; she likes the season's chicks and ducklings to pay their respects and ask her for a story, especially as lately they try to get out of it because she dithers on and on and backwards and forwards, and mumbles and never remembers what comes next."

"Oh dear," whispered Duckling, flinching at the prospect. The Literary Gander had not thought of Great-great-grandma-hen for a long time, but he held her in esteem, a truly Maeterlinckian character, though with some affinity to the atmosphere of Rostand's *Chantecler*— "Edmond Rostand, you know, not Jean. Jean is his son. Toad life is his speciality. I expect you see a good many toads round and about your stream. Do you know that the male toad frequently sings while mating? And that the female gets large fawn blotches under her arms to attract him at the right season? And that—"

This was truly terrible; he might go on about toads for ever. Duckling made a hasty excuse about having promised to be back in the Meadow before sundown, and escaped without much difficulty. He had gone two or three crooked paces when he turned back and asked: "Do you *really* think she would know lots about swans?" and without waiting for an answer, ran

away as fast as he had come, falling over several tus-
socks of grass before he disappeared into the overgrown ditch.

"Now I wonder what all that's about?" the
Gander reflected. "Swans on the brain! What could I
ever have said about them? Avon, Swan of; Proust,
Galsworthy, Pavlova—"

He wholly forgot the Danish-Legs.

The ancient Grandma Hen squatted in a trod-
den-down mess of many moultings, with pallid wattles
and red eyes, her dirty fawn feathers ballooning out
round her (just as Gander had described), receiving a
duty call from a cross, sullen chicken, driven unwill-
ingly to call on his matriarchal relative by his mother,
the White Hen.

"D'ye know what they call me? Speak up, I can't
hear you. What! You don't know? Great Auk, how
disgraceful! Pride of the Meadow; that's what they call
me. And how old d'ye think I am? Speak up, I can't
hear you. What, don't know?" (Neither did Grandma,
so that passed off all right.) "And what's your name,
eh? Ee all look so alike, I can't tell one from t'other.
What's that? What's that? 'Shan't declare'? Never heard
of it; newfangled name, that's what it is. Who's yer ma?
Eh, yer Aunt gave it to you, did she? And who might
yer Aunt be? Oh, *her*, with all them auburn feathers.
Thought as much. That's not their real colour; you
never get 'em as bright as that; she dyes 'em, just to get

the roosters to hang round. Don't you contradict me; all you smart young cockerels nowadays, always trying to teach your grandmothers to suck—to suck —to suck—what *is* it they suck?" Her wattles were flushed with anger, and it was just as well that Duckling came alone at that moment with a respectful: "How do you do, Grandma."

A swift glance of gratitude, and the chicken scuttled off, cheeping with delight at being freed from a burdensome interview.

"Please Grandma, you're so wise, and you've travelled so far and seen so much, may I ask you just one very small question, please, now or whenever you prefer? I can come along any time you like, please Grandma."

The old hen clucked with pleasure. These were the manners that suited her, deferential and sedate.

"When I was a little pullet," she began, "no bigger than you are now—ye be a pullet, bain't ye?" She peered with sudden suspicion at the small black shape with webbed feet, narrow head and long flat beak.

"No. No, I'm not a pullet; I'm only an ugly duckling."

"Never heard of 'em," with which Grandma settled the whole matter; and she composed herself for one of those sudden naps that helped to refresh her and keep her alive.

But when she woke up ten minutes later, Duckling was still there.

"Please Grandma, do you remember if you ever saw, before you came to the Meadow, a large wonderful beautiful white bird, oh, ever so beautiful and ever so much more glorious than any bird we ever saw here in the Meadow, called s–s–s–swan?" He stammered over the splendid beloved name . . . and waited tense with expectation until Grandma Hen should have ransacked the mildewy woods of memory.

It was a new experience for Grandma to be *asked* for her reminiscences; usually the young ones of the Meadow scattered in every direction to avoid them; so she was anxious to oblige. Being really of good birth and breeding, she had dwelt on the Home Farm of a Mansion where there were terraces, and on the distant

terraces, lordly birds could occasionally be glimpsed, spreading coloured fan-like tails and uttering raucous cries; birds that were held in high esteem by all the Legs of the Mansion. Doubtless the lordly ones were no more than a legend to the good homely little thing standing beside her and calling her "Please Grandma" so pretty. So from her fuddled brain she brought forth a fine mixture of birds and presented them to Duckling as the apocryphal swan. Their outstanding feature appeared to be a disposition to strut up and down terraces. No, she didn't think she'd ever seen 'em fly, and if she hadn't seen 'em fly, they *didn't* fly—Grandma's cackle rose shrill and angry, but relented on a hasty "No, no, of course not" from Duckling.

"Yes, come to think on it, some of 'em were white; not all, mark 'ee, but the best o't'lot. Aye, they thought a lot o' that swan, they did. Eh me, I can see thikky bird now, his tail spread out like the fans we used to carry with a nosegay of flowers when I was a young girl at a ball—let's see, two thousand, three thousand, eh, a mort o' days ago. And the roosters so smart in tail-coats and buttonholes. Eh dearie, dearie me" . . . Grandma subsided into a series of faraway cluckings and sighings . . . Once she lifted her voice in a few bars of the "Eton Boating Song," and presently fell asleep, exhausted.

But Duckling had slipped away, aware that he could get no more sense out of her. Anyhow she had told him more, much more than he had expected, and it was all wonderfully thrilling and glamorous; and to think that he himself one day would strut up and down terraces, spreading a tail behind him like a gleaming fan in the sunset. One or two oddments did not altogether fit in with what the Literary Gander had told him, who was, after all, the original source of scholarship and information, and must be believed when he related that all swans were white, and that swans flew, and that swans were silent until they raised their voices in a chant of unearthly loveliness just before death. So Grandma must have got a little muddled (and no wonder, at over 2,000 days old) when she had gabbled about their beautiful shrill voices like a train whistle just before it entered the tunnel at the railway cutting. That must have been some other bird, not a swan; the Literary Gander had said nothing about train whistles. Nevertheless, Duckling reflected gratefully, it had been good advice to go to old Grandma Hen, for she had added considerably to the compendium of swan data.

Terraces . . . Strutting up and down terraces. . . .

Six

"GRACIE'S A BOY TOO."

The Feeding Legs made her startling announcement, aware that it would create a sensation. "Our butcher's brother, him that comes round with the fish every second Thursday, he says there's no doubt about it, and he ought to know—he's had lots of kittens himself."

The Sardonic Legs decided this was a little too obvious for comment. As usual, the Nitwit Legs raised a wail: "Oh *dear!* Now we shan't know which of the three to keep if they're all boys. I'd tried to make up my mind that at least it mustn't be Gracie if you'd promise that she needn't be—you know; and we found a nice home for her where they didn't get angry if the sweet angel had kittens once a year."

"Baby, you're optimistic. Three times a year the sweet angel would have kittens. And don't talk about us as though we were a professional slaughter-house. We don't like it any more than you do—"

Nitwit Legs merely murmured: "I shall never get used to calling him anything but 'Gracie'."

"You needn't get used to it, if he's going to be sent away."

"But aren't you going to keep him, now she's a boy? If they're boys, why can't we keep all three?"

"They got to eat whichever they are," put in the Feeding Legs, who apart from practical considerations, *would* have liked to keep all three.

"It isn't between three, it's between two. You know we've done our best with Tiger Tim and it's no good."

Tiger Tim was the smallest, smoothest, slimmest, and plainest of the kittens, to whom Teazle, while still extant, had always allowed a double ration of milk. He missed his mother dreadfully, while Tony and Gracie hardly seemed to notice her removal, but went on healthily romping together.

"They're heartless, those two," said the Nitwit Legs, picking up Tim and petting him, while he nuzzled and pushed and burrowed into her puzzling anatomy, searching for milk. Everyone had been sorry for Tim, so palpably orphaned, so thin and different, so they had all picked him up and nursed and petted him . . . till they could not endure any longer his strange persistent endeavour to turn each one into Teazle; and more and more hastily they set him down directly his

fierce questing began on them. Till at last they had
ceased from picking him up at all.

"I'm sorry for the poor little goblin, said the
Owner Legs; "it really is pathetic, but he's uncanny; it
makes me feel as though at any minute I might grow
whiskers and a long bushy tall, and start washing my
face with my paw. He should have got used to doing
without her by now; and he gets far more than his
share of milk."

"I agree, Tiger Tim must go. It's between Tony
and Gracie-that-was, Georgie-that-is. It should be easy
to find a home for either Tony or Georgie, whichever
we don't keep."

The Feeding Legs, still standing by, put in a plea
for Tony as being the least greedy and most good-
tempered.

"What, Glamour Boy? Do we retain our Juvenile
Lead, dark handsome Adonis?"

"He lets me hold him any old way I like and
never minds. Look! Hanging upside down or on his
back." She demonstrated, and then let him drop to the
ground. Tony was glad to be released and bounded
away on rubber paws, but Tiger Tim appealed for
notice in his stead, and the Feeding Legs forgetfully
picked him up ... and a minute later dropped him
onto the knees of the Sardonic Legs ... who set him
down, also quite gently—they were all especially
gentle with Tiger Tim. "Beat it, you! I'm not what you
think. Honestly, he gives me gooseflesh."

Duckling, who was not far away, looked curiously to see what goose-flesh (which Tim had given the Sardonic Legs) was like; but nothing was apparent. He was sorry for Tiger Tim; for himself, he had no desire that the Legs should pick him up; nor had they ever tried; but he had watched the stripy smooth little body slink away over and over again, ostracised by the Legs, orphaned and forlorn; and in his heart a sort of affinity stirred and came to life. How well Duckling understood that he did not care to muck in with his family; Tim's two brethren were just like his own ten; but he and Tiger were different.

"That's odd. I've never seen a duckling follow a kitten before!" The Legs were a bit nervous over what might happen to Duckling.

Duckling found the little rejected cat lying in the earthy dark, under the raised verandah of the summer-house; he was remembering his mother and sobbing a little; at each sob his body heaved and sank, his tiger markings rippled.

"I wish you'd do that out here where I can see you properly," suggested Duckling, coaxing him by flattery into the open. "I've never seen such beautiful stripes."

Tim came out a little way . . . and then a little further.

Duckling lacked the comfortable amenities by which Tim's instinct might have striven to make a mother of him instead of a friend; therefore they were able, once they started, to enjoy a confidential chat, half hidden in the shade of the strip between the summerhouse and the garage wall.

"They call me Tiger; not altogether because of my stripes, but because of the way I move. They call me Tiger because—" he stopped, being fundamentally a modest little creature.

Duckling had an intuition— "Because of your fierce disposition?"

Tim was startled: "I say, how did you know?"

Duckling went from good to better, "I've *seen* them all being afraid of you."

"Have you? Have you really?" Then he could not be imagining it all, if this nice intelligent little duckling had noticed it too. "And you've seen them quickly push me away?"

"Hundreds of times. Legs are afraid of tigers."

"I'm not a tiger yet, but I'm not like the other two, am I?"

"Not a bit. They've got long fur and no stripes; and they gallop and play while you slink and ponder."

"Am I pondering?" in the gratified tone of Molière's Monsieur Jourdain on learning for the first time that he spoke in prose.

(No doubt but that Duckling and Tiger Tim encouraged one another.)

"Of course you are."

"Have all your brethren noticed it too? The ones that look like you and have such a jolly time playing up and down the stream. It's funny, but they never seem to mind getting their feet wet. Do you? Is that why you're hardly ever with them?"

"It isn't," Duckling proudly explained, "anything to do with minding about getting my feet wet. Don't be childish."

"I'm sorry," Tim said humbly.

"We may all look the same—*now*, but I'm absolutely and entirely and utterly and completely different."

"Different inside, you mean? Oh, I'm sure you are. I only—"

"Outside too, only it hasn't begun to happen yet."

Tim was beginning to feel a little bewildered, but he made a valiant effort: "Nor haven't I quite started to grow into a tiger yet. Once we do start, we'll be awfully quick, won't we?" How nice it was to be able to say "we," as he never could do with his brothers.

"Oh, as quick as quick. The Legs will run for their lives when they see you."

"And you? Will they run when they see you turn into whatever you're going to turn into when you start turning?"

"No," said Duckling dreamily. "They'll stand quite still and look up, higher and higher, right over the tops of the trees in the Meadow . . . With my fan spread out in the sunset, glistening, radiant, pure white."

Duckling had taken quite a fancy to Tim, and made a special long-distance journey over the road and ditch and through the slats in the fence and across the paddock of the Farm opposite, towards the upsticking shafts of the blue cart, where the Gander was usually to be found. For he wanted to consult his patron about tigers; and perhaps quench a lingering doubt as to whether he himself might not be indulging in fantasy, lost in a dream, victim of a delusion. "For facts are what matter," reflected Duckling, who was now a whole month older than when the Literary Gander had visited the Meadow and set him off.

Gander was interested in all he told him about Tiger Tim; and from his unending store of quotations, fished one up by a Poet Legs:

"Tiger, Tiger, burning bright
Through the darkness of the night,
What immortal hand and eye
Framed thy fearful symmetry?"

"Framed thy fearful symmetry," repeated Duckling, unselfishly delighted; for though he had no idea which part of a kitten its symmetry could be, he was very sure that that line especially would go over big when he recited it to Tim.

He lingered, however, for a moment still; "Then you wouldn't say that Tim had made it all up, about being something to do with a tiger?"—keeping back that item about the Legs being afraid of him, which somehow sounded a little silly when you took it right away from the garden and the Meadow, into a far territory.

"Oh, no; I wouldn't say for a moment that he had invented it. Cats do belong to the tiger species, you know, and it may be that your little pal has some genuine prenatal memory that dwells in his bones."

"Will it . . . come to anything?"

Gander surveyed him with an ironic yet indulgent smile which Duckling would have endured from no one else. "Run away home," he said; "you're getting out of your depth, you know."

"Out of my—?"

"Never mind; it's just an idiom we use when someone's drowning."

Now what had he said to send Duckling off like that, at full speed across the paddock and back to the safety of the Meadow? Too hypersensitive over some things, obtuse and almost dull about others. The Literary Gander, modern in his ideas, decided psycho-analysis was the thing for Duckling. Certain odd association words: swans, drowning, had produced extraordinary reactions. He felt a little lonely, as he often did since his Oxford days; his pals there would have understood and laughed had he remarked: "I expect when he was a few days old he saw something nasty in the woodshed."

Seven

At the end of August the helianthus in the herbaceous border at the wild end of the garden had grown taller than the trees; you could see them glow between the upper boughs. All the dahlias were out too, vivid and untrammelled. The Legs had had but little time to spare for weeding during those blazing summer days without rain, so that when Tiger Tim slunk about deep down among the stems in the cool places of monstrous swollen vegetation, they imagined he loved it because he was timid and it hid him; not aware that when they frequently referred to the "jungle," blaming themselves for it, yet too busy to cope, it set him off on his stripy, slinky prowl. The jungle framed his fearful symmetry as he crept about and rustled through dried-up Sweet Williams and other brown withered stems of the earlier summer plants. The Michaelmas daisies were out prematurely, in bushes almost as tall as the helianthus; while the smouldering berries of the prunus and a delicate second crop of honeysuckle and buttercups flourished in a bewilderment of seasons. A narrow path which ran alongside the border had been kept clear from the long encroaching orchard grass, otherwise no one could have pushed through. Apple-trees trailed their boughs heavily burdened with fruit, and a Victoria plum tree was loaded with ripening plums hanging down like a waterfall. In the exuberant clash of late summer against advancing autumn, bronze and gold were the prevailing hues; the unpollarded willows leant forward from the opposite side of the stream until they nearly touched the Cottage lawn; and gladioli, magenta and pink and orange and pale yellow, stood up in brilliant assembly in the round bed nearest the little terrace; thick purple and burgundy clematis twined and fell forward from its own weight on the walls of the Cottage; the narrow edge of marigolds and nasturtiums along the stream was being replaced by clumps of montbretia, orange bright among the leaning willows. In the rose-garden, where the Legs had supposed the wood strawberries were over, they suddenly began to appear again, moist and scarlet and more luscious than the June crop, as though they too had been infected by the season's riotous welter—

And the Attlee-Legs made a speech forecasting a hard and meagre winter with astringent ration cuts; and called on the country to produce all it could, store all it could, multiply wherever multiplication was possible. The ominous word "crisis" occurred frequently on the wireless; a winter crisis which had somehow to be fought before it arrived . . . And the Legs stared thoughtfully at the ducklings on the stream and the chickens clustered round the gate of the Meadow, and wondered when they would begin to declare themselves male or female.

The kittens provided relief from speculations that had perforce to be morbid and unloving. The kittens had been settled, sex and all, and those two who were left could be simply enjoyed, for Georgie-Gracie had already been sent to a good home in an adjacent county; while in a week or two, Tony was booked for a ten-and-sixpenny-worth at the vet (prices had gone up), and would then return in a demure and sobered condition, it was hoped, to remain unchallenged as the Cottage Cat. If still no home had been found for Tiger Tim (nobody wanted Tim, even though he was a male) then at the same time, he would have to be painlessly despatched to a not so adjacent county. . . .

"Oh, *don't!*" cried the Nitwit Legs, stopping her ears; but as the other two felt uncomfortable about it themselves, they displayed exasperation, as is the way of Legs:

"I never knew anyone like you who could keep on playing the same record over and over again. . . . We've heard all that about Tim. Tony's such a jolly contented purring, little fellow, he doesn't care a rap if he gets nursed or not, and would just as soon not"—

So they picked him up and nursed him, again as is the way of Legs, while Tim, who would have given his tiny soul for the chance, was for the hundredth time gently set down and told to run away and play in the jungle. "Sorry, Tim, but we can't keep two cats."

"They've got three over at Ruston Copthall."

"Poopsie happens to be a waif they've rescued from starvation; they're always hardest to get rid of when you've saved their lives and fed them with fountain-pen fillers. . . . In China, it's a law that you *have* to keep a man for the rest of his life when you do that."

"When you feed them with fountain-pen fillers?" Nitwit Legs' mouth opened in perplexity and did not quite close again . . . "Anyhow, a pure white kitten is somehow rare and exciting. I call her White Violet, not Poopsie."

"I expect Poopsie would prefer it. They all do. All the Poopsies."

An unaccountable twittering burst from the willow opposite where they sat. Hearing it, Tony sat upright and alert, ears pricked, body tense. . . .

"Oh, you *cruel* little cat! Look at him, he's licking his lips."

"I wonder," mused the Sardonic Legs, "how well *we'd* behave if all the rumpsteaks and fillet steaks and Porterhouse steaks up in the tree suddenly began to chirp and twitter?"

Tony struggled and flung himself free from the

restraining hand of his owner; leapt off his knees, then sprang back again and ran up onto his shoulder, and onto the next and nearest shoulder, and up a tree, and then off in chase of a wasp. . . .

"Don't be so wild and restless," the Sardonic Legs rebuked him. "Don't you ever sit down with a nice book?" Unfortunately Nitwit Legs did not understand his form of humour well enough to leave it at that. He had thrown open a door into Whimsy Castle, so she eagerly rushed in where even the bravest angel might fear to tread: "Oh, yes, he *does,* really and truly; you're all wrong; he's a shocking little bookworm, only he doesn't want us to know. In fact, if we were to creep up *very* softly and peep behind the sofa where he's always playing, perhaps we might find—"

"What are you all groaning about?" enquired a Learned Legs who had recently come to live at Brambleford, and enjoyed dropping in on the Legs at the Cottage.

"Nothing" . . . the Sardonic Legs subsided with a final glare at Nitwit Legs, who by now had sadly given up her intention of naming the authors of the supposed books to be found in the let's-pretend cat-library behind the couch.

"Watching your livestock, as usual?" The Learned Legs threw himself on the close-mown grass and lit a pipe. "I've never known such a *dolce far niente* crew in all my life. Hypnotised by ducks, that's you."

He had earned a storm of indignation, and got it!

They were all working harder than ever in their lives before ("I'd have you know"), and it was only in their very occasional intervals for recreation that they somehow gravitated to the lawn or on the terrace by the stream whence they could observe the antics of the little parasites. If you had not the luck to be a duckling yourself (what a care-free existence) the next best thing was to identify yourself with the duck world for an occasional half hour, and then return enviously to being a Legs, worried and cantankerous and heavily burdened.

The Learned Legs agreed lazily. "They *are* rather nice and ridiculous, your Team, Sord, Sute or Badelynge of Ducks."

Suddenly and to their great surprise, for hitherto they had thought of the Learned Legs only in proper terms of scholarship and distinction, he rolled over on to his face and broke into a recitation, delivered with illustrative gestures as he was taught in his youth, not at all dignified but quite amazingly agile considering his bulk and his years; every time he came to "*Up* tails all," he flung up his own backside with a jerk:

> "All along the backwater,
> Through the rushes tall,
> Ducks are a–dabbling,
> *Up* tails all!

Ducks' tails, drakes' tails,
Yellow feet a-quiver,
Yellow bills all out of sight
Busy in the river!

Slushy green undergrowth
Where the roach swim—
Here we keep our larder,
Cool and full and dim.

Everyone for what he likes!
We like to be
Heads down, tails up,
Dabbling free!

High in the blue above
Swifts whirl and call—
We are down a-dabbling
Up tails all!"

After a silence, the Owner Legs observed: "We haven't any roach." Which was cautious praise; indeed, hardly praise at all.

"I never said you had," the Learned Legs retorted, offended but not at all out of breath.

"You said it beautifully"; the kind-hearted Nitwit Legs could not bear him to think they had failed in appreciation. "I like the idea of the duck's larder, cool and full and dim."

"I wish ours were, in this weather," from the Sardonic Legs. "Did you scribble it yourself in one of your spare moments?"

The Learned Legs was too shocked to reply for several minutes; then in a hushed voice he told them a little—they did not deserve much—about a Legs of genius called Kenneth Grahame who years ago had lived about five minutes' walk away from the Cottage, just round the bend of the road where the chestnut trees left off, and opposite the pig-farmyard. You could tell the house by its wonderful japonica, and by the syringa that grew and bloomed all over the front of it; and behind was the garden; and behind the garden, the orchard; and at the end of the orchard the Stream . . . the same stream which flowed through their own garden. And sitting on the bank of this stream, he had thought of the *Wind in the Willows* and sent it along by instalments in letters to his little son who had been taken away on holiday but was so reluctant to tear himself from the adventures of Ratty, Mole, Toad, and Mr. Badger—

"You might as well say," he lashed himself into a fury again, and the top of his broad bald head was dangerously pink, "you might as well say you never knew that Lewis Carroll had been a Don of Mathematics at Oxford and was in reality the Rev. Dodgson . . . Or perhaps he was in reality Lewis Carroll?" he added, cooling down a little. "It depends what we mean by 'reality.'"

"We did know that," said the Nitwit Legs, who as a newcomer to the Cottage, had less need to apologise than the other two, "because we were told in the nursery; but you can't know things unless you *are* told, and nobody told us till now whose stream this was; but we'll *never* forget." Having a good but fitful memory, she repeated:

"Ducks' tails, drakes' tails,
Yellow feet a-quiver—

but the ducklings' feet aren't yellow yet. They haven't even begun to be."

Appeased by her rapid discipleship, the Learned Legs returned, like an earthquake settling down, to contemporary life on the stream:

"Which are ducks and which are drakes?"

But this was exactly what the Legs had not been able to decide, for they were waiting for that impudent little upturned quirk of feathers which grew on a drake a short way up its tail, which might not appear for at least three or four months.

"But you can tell by sound: the ducks quack full and free, and the drakes can only give out a small strangulated sound, as if they were beginning to say, 'There's no future in it.' And there *is* only an edible future for drakes. Sage and onions," began the Learned Legs, with relish, "and just a mere touch of lemon—"

The Owner Legs kicked him. And suggested to

73

Nitwit Legs that she should trip indoors and fetch some lumps of old crust and anything else she could find to throw to the flotilla and split them up; for they were moving about in such close and indistinguishable formation that it was impossible to tell which was making all the row rising into the still hot afternoon air. As though the ducklings had some notion of her errand, they drifted in close to the bank where the Legs were sitting or lying, and waited in confident expectation of favours.

"Can they hear?" the Owner Legs wondered. "Where *are* ducks' ears?"

"Dunno; never thought; they *can* hear; they know the food call and the rattle of the saucepan on the ground, and come tearing along."

With awakened interest they all closely scrutinised the smooth narrow heads. "I don't see anything sticking out," remarked the Sardonic Legs.

"You wouldn't expect them to stick out a mile like some people's ears?" The Nitwit Legs had rejoined them with a plateful of oddments, for once in time to get her own back with the Sardonic Legs. Aware of what some Legs had declared were the ruin of his air of sombre distinction, he dropped the subject and flung himself on the grass beside the Learned Legs, who was lying on his stomach in a listening attitude, with his head right over the water, the better to discover which duckling squawked in free full voice, and which were inhibited.

"Now, you two, chuck in what you've got. Good Lord, what's that pink muck?"

"Don't you remember it? It's the last of the jelly we had last week—or was it the week before? It was a failure, but it hasn't been thrown away. I suppose she couldn't bear to waste it. And I don't see why they should get nothing but horrid old bits of stale crust."

"So you brought them some lumps of old cold jelly. OK, fling 'em the crusts first, and we can listen to their loud disgust when it comes to the dessert course. Throw bits upstream and downstream so as to get them separated. Now!"

Followed a period of greed displayed by loud squawks and far-from-selfless squabblings and shovings and tearing through the water at the rate of small M.T.B.s, each duck striving to be ahead of the rest. ("It's not *fair;* I haven't had a bite for at least twenty minutes!" "Now you're chucking it all to him, and I was there first." "I'm starving—I suppose you Legs think we get all we want under the weeds. You'd be surprised; Aunts Donald, Dilly, and Dally pretty well cleared that larder before we were born; greedy-guts, that's what I call them, Aunt or no Aunt; greedy *and* common." "Quark, quark, quark! You do it on purpose: three huge bits running, just because he faked an itsie-bitsie pain in the crop. Aren't Legs *awful?*")

But all this was nothing to the storm of indignation which rose when the lumps of flabby pink jelly followed the bread.

"They're spitting them out." The Nitwit Legs spoke in tones of acute disappointment; in fact, she was very nearly crying.

"Hush, dear; you ought to be very glad to have helped us to find out they have a sense of taste and don't just gobble anything. Scientific research, you know. Interesting. Well?" The Owner Legs waited to hear the result of investigation as the two others scrambled up from their prone positions. "Surely they're all ducks, from the noise?"

"No; as far as I can pick up from their separate communications, only three are ducks—three or four; I'm not sure. And at least six drakes."

"But that makes only ten."

"There *are* only ten; I counted."

"No, eleven. I suppose little Stuff-and-Nonsense is moping somewhere apart, as usual."

"Look," said the Nitwit Legs; and pointed up the garden towards the little brick terrace outside the sitting-room . . . where Duckling waddled alone; up and down, following some obscure but consequential pattern of its fancy. None of the other ten ever walked on that side of the stream, and the Legs wondered at the temerity of the only one who never joined its brethren in the water.

"What *does* it think it's doing? Does it imagine it's a peacock?"

As though Duckling had understood, he paused in his perambulations . . . and with what seemed to be hard endeavour, slowly moved his tail from side to side, just as all the others did without any endeavour.

"Rum little beggar," remarked the Learned Legs. "Does it ever quack?"

"Not a sound."

"Oh, then it must be a drake. It's easy to tell with that one; sociable doesn't seem to be its middle name."

"Then if you're a drake, my little man," the Sardonic Legs began in accents of ghoulish geniality.

Tired of restraining him, the Owner Legs turned her attention back to the jolly flotilla in its natural element, still diving down hopefully for stray bits of the feast which might have got lost among the weeds; or else standing up on the tips of their tails like little penguins and flapping their wings furiously at the jelly-throwing Legs.

"Is canary-waistcoat one of the drakes? It was yellower when it first hatched out; I believe it's getting whiter."

"It looks as though it might have a strain of Sheldrake in it. They had a dopping of sheldrake on the pond at the farm opposite."

"Yes, before the new people moved in; there was a whole collection of exotic water-fowl, but we don't go there now, so I'm not sure if they're still there. A glorious sheldrake, all gold and orange, used to come over here when Donald, Dilly, and Dally were younger."

"That would be the Ruddy Sheldrake." It was

clear from the tone of the Learned Legs that he was using an official name for a certain species, and not merely indulging in his private opinion of it. "Did he come courting?"

"Unsuccessfully; I've never understood why; he was so handsome and romantic, but Donald, Dilly, and Dally fled in a panic for their lives, whooshing up the stream, hardly touching it."

"How sweet and maidenly; they must have been reading up their subject in one of those Bird Books for the Pocket: 'In courtship Drakes raise necks and dip them suddenly, walking round the Ducks. Short tussles.' I must bring you my bird book, it's most vivid and instructive. The Columba Panumbas, for instance, are monogamous. 'Drink freely. Gregarious in winter. Crops can hold sixty acorns. In courtship, male walks along bough or ground, bowing, cooing and raising tail; also aerial circling displays.' But the Columba Aeneas, on the other hand, though it also drinks freely, is 'tyrannical to female.' Lots of them are."

"*Quite* right," agreed the Sardonic Legs.

"One more"; the Learned Legs was clearly fighting temptation to recite the whole book.

"The Capercaillie—'In spring, cocks fight fiercely and, at dawn, perform a Spel (frenzied dance with wild, excited song), each in a favourite tree. Hens collect to admire.'"

"*Quite* right," repeated the Sardonic Legs, with even more emphasis; "mine don't," with a sad reproachful look towards the Owner Legs.

"Your little black fellows are Chinese Game Ducks, aren't they?"

"I believe so; the eggs were given us from the Manor, I think; but I can't quite remember. They're not really black if you look at them closely," for by now the ducklings had scrambled out of the water and were lying near the zinnia bed close by, energetically performing their toilets. "Some of their wing feathers are a sort of dark silvery brown, and there's a shimmer of blue and green and purple just beginning to show on them, but the general effect is black."

"I thought black ducks were Australian, not Chinese."

"You must be thinking of the Australian black swan."

None of them noticed that Duckling had stopped practising his peacock strut on the terrace, and had drawn close to them, paying an intelligent interest in what they said, palpitating at the mention of "swan," and bitterly disappointed when dropping the subject altogether as though it were of no special interest. The Learned Legs returned once more to contemplation of the ten black brethren spread in lumps and shapes on the bright green grass, some exhausted and half asleep, some fiercely slewing their necks right round, beaks plunged deep into their upper shoulders.

"An element of frenzy in the way they clean themselves, isn't there? One would think, being always in the water—"

Again the Learned Legs spoke with authority; they had always known he was a Learned Legs, but the encyclopedic variety of his information was really quite impressive: "They're not washing their necks, the same as we do every morning . . . some of us. They're spreading oil on their feathers."

"Oil?"

"Except in your own particular line, you're rather ignorami, aren't you?"

"Ignoramuses. And you're a pedant. Now enlighten us."

"You've heard the phrase 'like water off a duck's back'? In fact, you've seen it happen when you insult me, and your insult, instead of penetrating, rolls about on the surface and then falls off and I'm none the worse."

"Oh yes," agreed the Nitwit Legs, ignoring the human analogy and sticking to the ducks. "Of course I've seen them with their feathers glittering in the sun with diamond drops that the fairies save up and use for—"

"That's right. Those. And the reason their feathers don't get soaked with the water is because they spread their backs with oil; but the oily surface only lasts a couple of hours at the most; less when the birds are young. That's why they have to keep coming out to renew it."

"But where do they get it from, the oil?"

"From teeny *weeny* oil ducts," began the Sardonic

Legs unkindly, "all hidden away under their feathers, but they never speak of it as oil because as in the duck world that would be rudey-rudies, just as some of our natural functions mustn't be mentioned in polite society. They're taught to speak of it as their tiny treasure-trove."

The Nitwit Legs would have enjoyed the addition to the story, but mistrusted any parody from the lips of the Sardonic Legs. The Learned Legs, callous in a different style, illustrated the point by a rather sad little anecdote of a brood of ducklings who had somehow or other got into a derelict pond with high banks and could not get out again and swam round desperately seeking a landingstage, while their feathers from which the oil had rapidly evaporated became more and more heavily impregnated with water and they sank deeper and deeper and could no longer swim . . .

As Duckling's high destiny did not allow for any such form of on water-frolic (however tempting it might look on a hot day) he abandoned the society of the Legs and waddled across the lawn towards the plum tree where a nodding acquaintance of his, the moorhen, was trying to think out a feasible way of getting down the plums.

"I say, that isn't a duck or a drake over there? It's too small."

"That's our moorhen."

"Have you got many here?"

"Oh yes, quite a lot. They come up the stream from the farm opposite; under the bank round the island is their favourite camping-ground. There"s her mate, the moorcock. They adore plums."

The Learned Legs burst into song:

"The ousel-cock so black of hue
With orange-tawny bill"—

He debated silently whether he should go deeper into the nature of Shakespeare's ousel-cock, which emphatically, in spite of the bill's resemblance, was not a moorhen; then decided that he had perhaps been informative enough for one morning. The term "pedant" had not quite shaken off like water from his too unducklike back, but lingered and soaked in, as injustice so frequently does.

"I should love to marry a man called Tawny Bill," dreamed the Nitwit Legs.

"It might be managed; I'll look out for him."

The moorcock flew up into the top branches, and started to shake down plums to his mate, standing below to receive and be glad. The Legs were quite stunned by this virtuoso display, which for sheer audacity struck them as hard to beat. Did these urchins of the stream not realise that this was a *garden,* and that plums were *fruit,* and that the Legs, not they, were the owners of the plums, and that there was a hard winter ahead?

"The web-footed species is not renowned for tact; other fowl with space between their toes speak of being 'webfooted' with the same inflexion as we say 'thick-skinned.'"

"Can one *eat* moorhens?" asked the Sardonic Legs.

Intent as ever on his quest, after exchanging a few ordinary civilities with the plum-glutted Moorhen, Duckling asked: "Tell me, do *you* think there's something very special and wonderful about being white?" (*Not* renowned for tact. . . .)

The Moorhen replied with twinkling eyes: "Special is as special does; the whole garden is full of Cabbage Whites, huge flocks of them; haven't you heard the Legs complain? One would think from the way they carry on, that they reckon to eat nothing else but cabbages this winter."

"Oh, I wasn't thinking of butterflies. There are millions of them, and they all look exactly alike." Duckling was properly contemptuous of such poor white trash. "No, I was thinking of Auntie Donald. You know my Auntie Donald, don't you?"

"I know all three of 'em. They don't like me, but have to put up with it when I whistle through my fingers and call out remarks as they swim past the island."

"Is our island your home?"

"I've a dozen homes. Sleep anywhere; mostly over opposite."

"Auntie Dilly and Auntie Dally are brown and fawn; they don't count. Auntie Donald always swims a little ahead of them; always first, never last. She's white, you see, and they, the Legs, were hinting just now

about something exciting that had happened to her and not to the others. I think they said it was *because* she was white."

"Go on; don't mind me," laughed the Moorhen. "I can tell you one thing that did happen to your Auntie Donald and not the others, and that was the time the Sheldrake flew over; the only time, I believe."

"That's it! That's it!" cried Duckling, thrilled at having struck the spoor so rapidly. "Was it the Ruddy Sheldrake?"

"Yes, ruddy as anything. He flew over here from my part of the world, down stream. None of us know where he's got to now, though his parents are still with us; they don't fly, or can't, I'm not sure, but their son was always flying and he'd set his heart on your Auntie Donald—if heart's what you call it"—and the Moorhen, with a low taste in jokes, gave a smutty snigger. If the Brown Hen had been anywhere handy, undoubtedly she would have called Duckling away from this undesirable little companion he had picked up under a plum-tree—"with the tongue of a street arab and the morals of a night-club". . . . And in very fact, there she was on the opposite side of the stream, beckoning and clucking like mad, expressing the utmost agitation and disapproval; but as the hens seldom if ever crossed the bridge higher up from the Meadow into the garden, of course Duckling took no notice whatsoever, but went on earnestly soliciting information to add to his private store.

The little Moorhen began to whisper, tawny bill close to Duckling's ear: "It was one of our few warm evenings last summer, and suddenly there he stood in the patch of rough grass over the willows on yonder side. I'd have thought any duck would have been glad, especially those three who had never had so much as a *smell* of a drake, that I know of. I'm sure if he'd asked me I'd not have said 'No,' though I wasn't out yet. Prince jewel, I used to call him; Great Roc alone knows who his father was! I heard the Legs gossiping about it; they said he wasn't quite pure—I'll lay he wasn't. Well, there he stood just looking and looking at your white duck, and all of a sudden, as if he'd been cut loose from a sort of spell, he made a rush towards her—(they'd just been waddling off towards the Meadow gate thinking only of their crops as usual; the Feeding Legs was there). But when Donald saw the Sheldrake she screamed like a dying Legs in a thunder-storm and hurled herself into the stream, the Sheldrake after her like a streak of flame. You never heard such a swishing and a squawking. He got our Donald down under the water . . . one would have thought she was being murdered. Her two sisters rushed up to rescue her, and between the three of them they chased the unwelcome suitor right down the stream and out. Between you and me, I'm not so sure Donald was as pleased about that as she had to pretend to be. Comes of overdoing the Victorian act. As far as I know, she's never had another offer, if offer's what you call it"—

and once again the Moorhen gave that rude and regrettable snigger, and the Brown Hen from the opposite bank squawked more frantically than ever, calling her pseudo-offspring home. She need not have worried; most of this was over Duckling's head, intent upon his own fantasy. The bit he extracted from all that welter and laid aside for future recollection was that the *white* one of the three aunties had been singled out; the other two left. He sank into a reverie . . . and the Moorhen, bored and replete, departed in a series of little hops and one loud hoarse derisive squawk directed towards the brown mother hen as she reached the island.

   . . . And only *one* pure white gladiolus, mused Duckling; all the rest orange and pink and magenta. And only one white hen among the multi-feathered and undistinguished Meadow crowd of hens. Incurably stupid and conventional, with a wood-pigeon coo in her voice, she always greeted Duckling with: "Well, dear, had a nice swim?" or "Was it nice in the water to-day?" or "Going in for your dip?," never having noticed that this particular Duckling did not go in the stream; for they were all alike to her: "Your brood of little funnies," she would remark amiably to her younger sister, the Brown Hen. "Eleven! Well, well! And as like as peas in a pod. I hope they'll be a comfort to you one day, as my chickabiddles already are to me."

   Nevertheless, the white hen *was* white, therefore

different from the rest, therefore the Legs knew her and singled her out when the Feeding Legs came back from the henhouse with a basket: "White Hen laid this one," she would say; or: "White Hen hasn't laid to-day; I watched to see if she's gone back to her old place in the hedge, to lay it there; don't mind as long as we know. But she's having a day off; no sign anyhow of her going broody again, though some of the rest are looking that way."

The one white duck, the one white hen, the one white gladiolus . . . and the legend of White Violet. White Violet belonged to the Ruston Copthall Legs who had once come over and sat where Duckling could hear her animated voice in narrative of how she had rescued two starving little kittens from a big barn where they had been left to die, and fed them and nourished them and had found a home for the ginger one, but the smaller and more dying of the pair was pure white, not a fleck on her, so of course she was kept, for a pure white kitten was unique and could never be mistaken for a whole lot of cats running about the garden. Duckling had indeed suggested to Tiger Tim, in a burst of warm-hearted match-making, that here for him was a fitting bride, and would he like him to start getting busy about an introduction? But Tim retorted proudly: "A tiger chooses his own jungle mate!" The Ruston Copthall Legs frivolously alluded to this shining specimen as Poopsie; but the Nitwit Legs, who at fleeting moments could claim understanding, always spoke of her as White Violet; millions of other violets in the garden, blue and mauve, but only one very feeble plant that had to be coaxed and sheltered, and you could always tell it from the rest at a glance: "white violet" . . . Was there somewhere removed from taint or blemish, from the mob of common hues all thrown together anyhow, a royal kingdom where white alone existed? And did it send forth every now and then into the jarring clashing world of colour, a haunting reminder of how white whiteness could be?—a white duck, a white hen, a white gladiolus, a little white cat, a white swan . . . A pure white swan.

During this senseless period of his exile due to his puzzling miscarriage into a family of little black squawkers, Duckling was seized with an impatient desire to speak to one of his own kind.

Auntie Donald was now bathed in glamour; he would seek out Auntie Donald with some friendly little overture such as: "Do you know, I can never tell Auntie Dilly and Auntie Dally apart; they're as like as two peas in a pod; but of course you're different, you're *white*"—And by that action he would become Auntie Donald's favourite, and they would go off together and sit under the white gladiolus and eat white bread— "I'm not going to give you fowls white bread so don't you think it and it's no good coming pecking round me," the Feeding Legs had said one day, shooing them away from the kitchen door. "There's a saying everybody eats white bread once in their lives, but it don't apply to ducks!" ("And may I ask why not?")

Still, "white" again! Evidence. So after the radiant hour of his metamorphosis, every now and then he would spare a moment to fly back to the Meadow World and be very very kind to old white Auntie Donald.

Duckling was a little hazy as to how he would slough his present disguise, cast off obscurity and take wing into that fair white kingdom of his Swanage. Swan-upping.

... The Legs, sitting with *The Times* on the terrace the other morning had paused at a photograph on the back page: "Look, swan-upping!"—but not with bated breath as would have been right and reverent. Insensitive Legs! Duckling had found it impossible to procure a copy of *The Times,* though he had gone all round the newspaper shops, tantalised by the premonition of himself in graceful flight, higher and higher, upping and ever upping into the celestial blue. ...

Donald, Dilly, and Dally were nonchalantly gossiping of this and that, in the cool shade of the mint bed near the kitchen door. There was a certain pleasure in grumbling about the Legs so near their own domain, for in sooth they did not think much of any Legs, and had drawn into their little circle Rhoda, the flighty hen, after a vain attempt also to lure the goose from her husband's side.

"Me and my sisters have resided with these Legs for a long time now. Gave us such silly names before they *knew*. . . And why *didn't* they know, that's what we should like to know? *We* knew. Donald, Dilly, and Dally indeed.

We registered a strong protest and demanded they should be changed to Donna, Dahlia, and Daffodil; but no, they wouldn't play, and if the Legs don't set an example to the Meadow, how can you ever expect—"

At this point they were interrupted: "Auntie Donald!" A small black duckling had waddled round from the terrace and was standing beside them, toes well turned in, head held a little on one side in an ingratiating fashion.

"Auntie Donald!"

The white duck favoured him with a cold hard stare: "I'm no ruddy relation of yours. Make yourself scarce."

"I *am* scarce," replied Duckling haughtily; then, remembering his quest, caught at the operative word and continued pleadingly: "Oh *please,* Auntie Donald, won't you tell me all about what happened when the Ruddy Sheldrake came over to see you?"

Eight

"Say, come down. There's been a letter." The Sardonic Legs summoned his companions from different parts of the cottage.

"Anything wrong?"

"Those confounded ducks!"

"Have they turned up?" For the flotilla had been missing for two whole days, so the Owner Legs was relieved at the idea that their whereabouts was discovered.

"They've turned up, yes, but on the wrong side of the road; they're over there, and how we're going to get them back—" he handed them the letter in which "Over There," curtly and not at all in a neighbourly manner, had complained of the ducks who were trespassing on his land, and would the owners kindly attend to the matter, as they were being a nuisance, and if they could not be kept under control, the right place for them was shut up in a wire enclosure on their own field.

"What an ogre!" exclaimed the Nitwit Legs, standing behind the Owner Legs where she had sat down on the steps of the little terrace, and reading over her shoulder.

They all felt more disturbed than they cared to own; disturbed and helpless. How were eleven ducks— no, ten; Little Stuff-and-Nonsense was clearly to be seen dreeing his own weird just across the bridge— how were ten lively young ducks, heady with a jocund liberty hitherto unquestioned, to be enticed home from gambolling in unspecified localities of pond and stream and sedge in somebody's else's ground? And even if you succeeded in luring them back, how were they to be kept back?

"You can't *tell* ducks to stay where they're well off in their own garden," said the Owner Legs; "at least, you can, but they don't listen—much. Nobody minds them up the other way of the stream, under the culvert and where it runs past the cottages; they like them there, and feed them; so why do these infernal little brutes choose to go where they might have known they were not welcome! Still, they can't be doing much harm, can they?"

"Ten ducks have a pretty good nuisance value to a man who doesn't happen to be infatuated with them, as you are. And if one has to put up with a whole bunch of them messing up the shaven lawn just in front of the drawing room windows, one might conceivably prefer them to be one's own little pets. We would!"

"But he can't really *mean,* can he, that we were to keep them shut up in the Meadow, behind wire, not able to get out into the water or to be happy ever again? He *can't* have meant it."

"I don't know. . . . People are different."

They were all silent, thinking of the cool shadowy Eden up and down the stream and among the drowned willowroots; the alluring prospect (for ducks) of dipping deep into the weeds for morsels of succulent booty to the finder; of chasing and splashing, scattering fountains of shining drops; those absurd webbed feet (getting yellower now) paddling away like mad; a day-long ecstasy of freedom and celebration.

"Look here," the Nitwit Legs broke out suddenly, for she could guess without any telling that the imaginations of the other two functioned in the same way as her own over really important matters, "he hasn't thought of all that. Suppose I were to run across and tell him? I'm not afraid; I'd describe what ducks do in the water, and how it would feel to be cooped up quite near it, still able to see it and smell it and hear it . . ."

The Sardonic Legs and the Owner Legs did not burst out laughing, and ridicule the notion of the Nitwit Legs sitting down to a cosy chat with the Ogre Legs, enlightening him in her own enthusiastic whimsical idiom as to just how ducks would feel in captivity. It could not be attempted, of course, for in her own way she might appear as insistent a nuisance as the ten trespassing ducklings rolled into one; but she escaped a snubbing, and the Sardonic Legs remarked quite kindly: "These are methods which if they could be applied all round, would prevent war ever happening to us again."

"Then may I?"

"No, my dear, you mayn't."

"But you've just said that if one did, it would stop war."

"I know; but all the same you mayn't."

"Why?"

"Because something would have to happen first that is known, I believe, as a change of heart."

The Owner Legs agreed. "That's exactly it. And one gets so horribly discouraged. I tried your methods once with a couple of film directors, but it was no good; they referred me to their Legal Department, which from my point of view was absolutely beside the point. I wanted them to play ball; I wanted them to talk turkey. But they kept on being suspicious that I meant to trap them. Then I tried it again over a man whom I wanted to meet just once, only to put something right that had gone as wrong as it could go—"

The Nitwit Legs was diverted from the urgent present to ask: "And wouldn't he talk turkey either?"

"No. Also suspicious of the hidden motive."

"So one goes to war?"

"So one goes to war."

The Nitwit Legs sighed, and returned from intangible turkeys to ten very tangible ducks:

"Then what are we to do?"

"We don't know. It's a bad world for men of good will."

The Feeding Legs was summoned; and to their infinite relief the Riding Legs, who had been away on some horsey business, appeared with her. There was no need to relate more than briefly what the Ogre Legs had written in complaint of the ducks; for the Riding Legs had already been in communication with the Handy Legs from over the road, and was full of bits and pieces of news:

"They're in a fine state across there; got trouble of their own; all comes at once. Two of their ducks, valuable ones they bought with the place, went off together—"

"And they don't belong together," put in the Feeding Legs with relish. "The female, she's a—what do you call it? Like the one came over here after Donald, Dilly, and Dally."

"The Sheldrake," shouted all three together. And the Nitwit Legs added, proud of knowledge recently acquired: "The Ruddy Sheldrake."

"Oh, he was, was he? Well, it was that one's mate, the female; she's been and escaped with the Paradise Sheldrake. They got right up to the path going Topley way before they were caught and brought back. Good thing, with so many foxes about."

"Go on," continued the Feeding Legs, nudging him to remember. "Tell them what Bobby Stone found in the tree."

Apparently an Urchin Legs, while seeking a little too thoroughly for the eloping pair in hope of the reward promised for them alive or dead, thrust his hand in a hollow tree that lay across the ditch not far from the estate; had touched something soft . . . and brought his hand away dabbled with blood from the body of the rarest duck from the previous tenant's collection. She too had strayed, and been shot by some prowling Gun Legs. Afraid of discovery when he saw what he had done, he must have stuffed the body in the hollow tree and hoped for the best.

"Oh, *do* let's get our own ducklings back quickly," cried the Nitwit Legs, thoroughly disturbed at all these dramas of bodies and bloodshed. Then suddenly veering round: "No, don't let's get them. I couldn't bear to see them shut up and miserable, with their beautiful shining wings all draggled and dusty. I'd rather they—Oh, I don't know *what* I'd rather, except for it to stop being such a horrid morning."

But the recent burst of added respect shown her by the other two, had already passed off. They now snubbed her, snapped at her, jumped down her throat, and metaphorically threw her down and rolled her in the mud; bade her shut up and not make an ass of herself; demanded what the hell use was it to whimper and carry on over a lot of rotten maddening troublesome little ducks that would be far better on a plate served with sage and onions, the lot of them, male and female alike—

"I heard your voices the whole way down the lane," remarked the Learned Legs, "or I wouldn't have dropped in during your working hours. What's wrong?"

They told him, all five of them together, so that he received a rich variety of impressions and opinions. And the Riding Legs added that he might put on his great rubber waders and once more see what could be done to get 'em back, and then while the wife fed 'em, he'd rig up some wire netting across that end of the stream, too strong for them bothering ducks to get past, and let 'em stay in the water in their own garden and plenty good enough too. He marched off with a purposeful air.

The Learned Legs looked at his watch: "Not yet ten o'clock, but bring me beer. I was out with the search party last night, and haven't recovered my regular habits."

The Feeding Legs bustled off. And the Nitwit Legs exclaimed: "Oh, then you found the Paradise Sheldrake who had gone off with the Ruddy Sheldrake's mate? What does a Paradise Sheldrake look like? Had he a wife of his own?"

"The Paradise Sheldrake is dense black. His mate is gold and black. . . ."

"His grieving mate," sighed the Nitwit Legs, flooding sympathy over whatever was happening to anybody in the duck line. "But how beautiful the other two must look together, dense black and ruddy gold. Did they seem happy?"

"Madly. But not so happy to be picked up and brought back home. Passion is strong. . . . And they've gone off again."

"Again! Then they're not over there, and I was going to ask if I might see them."

"Ask whom?" And at the grim note in the Sardonic Legs' voice, the Nitwit Legs blenched; she had forgotten that a merry state of come-and-go existed no longer between the Cottage and the Farm Opposite. The Learned Legs had however not yet heard the extra tragedy of the Mandarin Duck, and it really upset him.

"They're such lovely little things, and the rarest of the whole bunch. She was quite small, not much bigger than a moorhen, gold and green with a sort of white plimsol line all round her body just about where it would reach the water when she swam, and a dark green plume on her head. But the thrilling thing about the Mandarin Duck is the orange feather that doesn't lie down when she closes her wings, but rises up along her back like a little sail. They're kept as pets in China: Royal Mandarin Ducks."

. . . Duckling listened with his heart beating wildly, and a curious blend of jealousy and sorrow; jealous because the Mandarin Duck had been acknowledged as rare and royal and beautiful, transcending all other ducks; sorrow for her untimely fate.

"If I were ever a Paradise Sheldrake"—("Seems unlikely," muttered the Sardonic Legs, but the Nitwit Legs took no notice)—"I'd fly away with the Mandarin Duck instead of with Mrs. Ruddy Sheldrake. Do you think it was her husband or her son who came over here wooing Donald, Dilly, and Dally?"

"Only Donald," the Owner Legs corrected her. "It was before your time."

"That would have been the son," the Learned Legs spoke with authority. "If he flew over, she must have gone astray before now, and brought in a strain of wild duck. None of these can fly; they've been pinioned so that they shouldn't."

"Pinioned? But we've seen them from the distance, running about."

He explained the process of pinioning. "It means snipping the tiny muscle that lifts the wing on the left side; that's quite enough; it doesn't hurt, nor prevent them from making any other movements; only they can't rise, or if they do, they just go round in a short circle and have to come down again."

Duckling repeated to himself: "The tiny muscle that lifts them . . . so that they can't rise. Oh, how cruel! Surely, surely they would never dare do that to a royal swan? But a swan would never allow them to approach near enough to have the chance."—And standing unnoticed on the terrace, for the hundredth time he tried to force his whole strength to become aware of a tiny muscle that would lift him and carry him high up and away. . . . Not yet, not yet, but no need for despair; he must be patient.

Suddenly to become conscious of the muscle that could lift you only if you *were* conscious of it—was it like falling in love?

"So they *ran* all the way, nearly to Topley? We thought they'd flown. What a shame to bring them back, but how nice that they've escaped again."

"You're all for a lawless career, are you? What about our own ten young ducks?"

Precisely in time to answer the query, the Riding Legs reappeared in waders and with no news. "I went as far as I could, rattling the saucepan, but I never even caught a glimpse of them. They must be beyond that old tangle of shrubs and trees where the stream joins the pond. No use putting up the wire till they do get back, or it'll keep 'em out."

The Owner Legs' glance happened to stray towards Little-Stuff-and-Nonsense standing near, *pro tem* the sole and faithful remnant of the whole flotilla. An irrational exasperation suddenly shook her: "I do think it's a frightful little prig not to have gone off with the others!"

They all agreed.

The flotilla returned by water; returned of their own accord, at sunset when the Legs were out, and as full of their adventures as (by a Shakespearean idiom not much used in the Meadow) an egg is full of meat. During their three days' truancy they had seen and heard so much which was new and sensational that, wholly free from any disturbing sense of guilt, all they cared about was to dash up to somebody, anybody, and burst forth with their thrilling narrative. The first person they saw, scratching round the bank of the stream on the Meadow side, happened to be the White Hen, whom roughly speaking they took to be their mother; for by now, independent young fellows of three months old, they had lost even a shadowy instinct of attachment towards the brown hen who had hatched them; and whenever they saw a similar shape, dimly recognised it as something they had once been taught to call "Mummy."

"Well, darlings," clucked the White Hen, charitably aware of a need to be kind to her sister's odd little changeling brood; "are you going to have a nice bathe? Is the water cold?"

They all began quacking in chorus, so that it was some little time before she could fish out any clear idea of the subject of so much excitement; but when she became aware that their gleeful narrative actually revolved round an elopement in the duck world, in circles she and her sisters had decided long ago it were better not to recognise, her virtuous feathers stiffened, and she said thank you she didn't wish to hear any revolting details about this Lord Paradise who had run away with the Ruddy Sheldrake's wife; she would never allow *her* chicks to be mixed up in such matters even at second or third hand; and if that was what entertained them, then all she could say was had no one ever told them they mustn't repeat scandal? And they had thoroughly dirty little minds, but what could you expect? ... With which cryptic utterance she turned and pecked her way with an offended air back to the hen-house in search of her sister, the Brown Hen. But the Brown Hen was laying at the moment; and so by all the laws of the Meadow World (and indeed, of the Legs' world) must be protected from agitation till she had done her bit.

The ten did not much care that they had made a mistake; only that their first fine careless rapture was checked for want of a receptive audience; where *was* everybody on this evening of all evenings, when they had such lots to tell? So next, and with only slightly diminished confidence, they charged up to the Military Gander, a long way across the Meadow; and started this time at the wrong end of their escapade, treating him to a cheerful conceited account of how indispensable they had been through the hurlyburly of passion, horror, grief, murder, and sudden death which had descended in spate on the region near by, leaving the protagonists helpless as characters in a classical tragedy (this was not exactly how the ducks put it, but near enough). They themselves had not been at all overwhelmed, so were of the greatest imaginable help, tearing to and fro in everybody's way, scuttling under the very feet of the Ogre Legs, quickly scooping up a share of the corn thrown on the ground as there were now three less—"we haven't told you about the murder yet"—and some might otherwise be wasted; following the search party with loud quacks, so as to warn and startle away the couple for whom the search-party was searching; acting on a bright idea of interviewing Lady Paradise Duck and asking her if she could give them a few words (not more than six or seven hundred) on how it felt to be forsaken—

The Military Gander gave vent to his feelings in a succession of oaths enough to intimidate any young ducks less delighted with themselves than this particular badelynge at this particular moment. "Reporters! Scum! Vermin! A rotten prying inquisitive lot of ghouls! By Gad, I suppose if I were to die in some heroic engagement in defence of the Meadow, you wouldn't even leave my dear goose alone to relieve her overcharged liver by a few quiet tears, without a dozen of your kind nooping round the scoop—no, scooping round the noop, snooping round the coop—that's it, snooping round the coop for the sake of a few miserable shillings! If I had my way I'd horsewhip the lot of

you, and give you 28 days C.B. into the bargain.
Publicity!"—From an excess of wrath he choked; then
stretched forth his neck in a long horizontal line and
hissed and hissed with such vehemence and staying
power that even the gaggle of ten thought they might
as well go in search of someone else; for as far as they
could see, Gander was unlikely to prove a hushed and
attentive listener, nor be impressed in quite the right
way by what he heard.

So a little disappointed but not noticeably, they

returned to the stream at the mint and kitchen end. Perhaps a spot of refreshment might be available if they clustered round the kitchen door; it was nearly half an hour since they had thrust their ten intrusive beaks among the food allotted to the ducks and poultry on the estate over the road.

And near the kitchen door they ran into the only one of their own close kin who had not been in at the death, nor at the elopement, nor witnessed any of the lovely lovely *lovely* things which had happened at the Farm Opposite, while life here at the Cottage and the Stream and the Meadow had gone on in its old humdrum way.

Poor Duckling had to hear it all, and probably far more than had he actually been in their company making ten into eleven. They spared him nothing, and would have given a complete news commentary had not the Riding Legs, less by honeyed words than by sight, sound, and smell of succulent food, tricked them into the shed. Where they were kept shut up and in disgrace till strong wire netting had been laid across the stream at the upper end of the garden. "As cunning as a wagonload of monkeys, they are."

But the Nitwit Legs took no part in the triumph, the capture and the barricading. Removed from busyness, she squatted on the steps of the terrace, dreamily floating flat nasturtium leaves down the empty stream . . . and irrelevantly thought of an anecdote told them by the Learned Legs: The story of a teal, brown on top like a mallard, and lovely light blue underneath its wings, whose nest he had found in among the reeds on the water when he had been living in East Anglia; very carefully he had taken the eggs to put them under a Silky Bantam—good hatchers who would sit for a long long time—but the little teal, in great distress, ran alongside him pecking at his trousers.

It was a legend of no importance or size, but somehow, after three pink gins at the Pig and Whistle, it seemed to epitomise all the inarticulate sorrows of all the world.

Not far away from her, in a clump of tall grasses, Duckling also squatted alone, and also a prey to melancholy. The Mandarin Duck was dead; the Royal Mandarin Duck, they called it in China; a crumpled shape, limp and lifeless, hidden in a hollow tree; wantonly murdered, its vivid green and gold feathers dim and dabbled with blood. The Mandarin Duck, the only one, the rarest of them all. How strange, how romantic to be rare, to be special, to be different, not to be ordinary; to bring forth paeons of praise, or better still, the silence of sheer wonder. . . . "A hush fell on the Meadow and the Stream, and they realised for the first time that the homely little creature who had moved amongst them for so long, patiently bearing its disguise till its hour had come, was not only a swan but a Swan of Swans, the second Royal Swan to come down from Avon. And the Swan soared up and up and beyond the flock of little golden clouds, still higher into the blue Avon, and never never returned to the Meadow where they had looked on him as being only one of eleven ducklings, exactly the same as the rest, not even uglier. . . ."

"Hello!" said the Nitwit Legs. "How did you get away from the shed? Or are you little Stuff-and-Nonsense? I'm never quite sure."

Bitterest of all that even the Nitwit Legs, who fool though she was, had hitherto recognised by some faint stirrings of discernment that Duckling possessed a quality different from the rest, that even she should not be sure!

Nine

DUCKLING'S DISTRESS WAS INCREASING, that he was not more noticeably ugly. Or perhaps he was and his brethren had made no comment; the ten were not observant. If he believed the Gander, and he did, ugliness was an essential of his future transformation into Swan. He sought to make them notice his looks on the comparatively rare occasions when they all met on land; but they refused to be shoved into the role of persecutors; nor were they mirror-conscious for themselves; though all their chatter was water-chat, the multiplying reflections swaying on the broken willow-shadows evoked no Narcissism. Vanity and languor go together, and they were too gay and greedy to be vain. Duckling felt more hope in the Legs remarking on his ugliness, and to that end he hung around them more than ever when they were out-of-doors, and once tried to push his way into the Sardonic Legs' ground floor study, jabbing the door open with his beak. If only the Sardonic Legs could be provoked into saying: "Why! It's our ugly duckling who grows uglier every day; definitely more so than the other ten. It's really quite remarkable. Surely there must be a reason for so conspicuously ugly a duckling, though ponder as I may, I cannot discover what that reason is!"

Unhappily the Sardonic Legs was a very stupid Legs, an engrossed-in-earning-his-living Legs; he did just glance up at what was perhaps the slightly unusual sound of an embarrassed "Quark" over by his book-case; murmured an absent-minded welcome: "Hullo, Stuff-and-Nonsense!" . . . and returned to his writing.

A dejected Duckling waddled out again into the brilliant sunshine, and wished impatiently for some-thing to do that might help to pass away the time.

He was hardly a duckling any more. None of them were. At three months old you came of age. A burnish of green and blue began to appear on the heads of two and then three and then four of his brethren, and a flab of brighter hue on their wings, especially brilliant when the sun stabbed through the willows and picked out the turquoise and the emerald feathers. Breathlessly excited at any development in the appearance of his kin (character did not matter, and indeed they had none to speak of), Duckling won-dered whether precisely the same beauty had begun to brighten his own head and underwings. If so, all was lost. He tried, by standing on the bridge and bowing his head as low over the stream as he actually dared without tumbling in, to peer at his own reflection,but the weeds sprawled along the surface and all was weed-green.

(What on earth's little Stuff-and-Nonsense doing now? Surely it can't be going to dive, after all these months?) He was just on the verge of paying a call on the Literary Gander by his own overland route, when Holly's Legs ran in with a basket of early plums, and cried out with enthusiasm at the sight of the glimmering peacock hues—("What's a peacock?" Duckling wondered) —on four of the flotilla who were lying on the bank, their necks slewed round, their beaks burrowing for oil. She added: "And look, I believe it's coming on that one too. Are they all going to be like that?"

"No; only the drakes. That little one's quite plain and dull, and so's that one, and that one"—

For a wonder, Duckling was not far away and could be counted in without having to seek him right up towards the terrace or the bridge—"And *that* one," added the Sardonic Legs with hardly a pause.

Plain and dull. Good. That meant ugly.

But discontent returned. For three of the others were counted off in the same category. And of what use to be one among four Ugly Ducklings? This was persecution of a particularly subtle nature; they must know that no ill-treatment was so tormenting as indifferently lumping him in.

"Can you be sure that those glorious ducks are the drakes?" asked Holly's Legs, it seemed regretfully.

"Fraid so," said the Owner Legs. And for at least the fiftieth time, the Nitwit Legs cried out: "Oh, *don't!* I can't bear it! We don't *have* to, even if they are drakes?"

"It needn't be just yet." Thus the Owner Legs tried to soothe her. And the Sardonic Legs explained quite kindly: "We couldn't keep a lot of drakes for show, even if we wanted to; I mean, even if it weren't for the Winter Shortage—"

"I hate those words," broke in the Nitwit Legs. "They always lead to murder and worse."

"Now what can you possibly mean by 'and worse'?"

The Nitwit Legs meant cannibalism.

"Bilge! Cannibals eat their own kind."

"They don't; cannibals never eat cannibals." (Long ago, Duckling had lost interest in this absurd conversation.) "They eat innocent confiding white men." At the magic word "white," his attention was caught, and he moved a little nearer so as to miss nothing. "And black ducks *are* white men to us, so there you are." (Now what could even a really well-educated and intelligent Duckling make of that: "Black ducks are white men"? Would even the Literary Gander be able to extract from it a particle of sense?)

"What I was going to say fifteen minutes ago, before you began to gargle sentiment," the Sardonic

Legs spoke with deceptive patience and lucidity, "related to the biological fact that if you keep for decorative purpose seven drakes and four ducks, the ducks are liable to receive rather too overwhelming attentions from the males."

"But that's nice for them," cried the Nitwit Legs. Holly's Legs laughed merrily.

"Furthermore," the Sardonic Legs continued, having recently strolled up and down the lawn with the Learned Legs and benefited by his erudition, "it is more than probable that all the seven drakes would fasten their ardent fancy on one duck out of the four who to us would look more nor less desirable than its three sisters. And that duck, my girl, would die a horrid death. Horrider even than with sage and onions, green peas and new potatoes."

"So that whatever we do about it, it'll come to the same thing in the end? Well, I don't believe it. I believe that man invented it all because he hoped to be asked to dinner. He's a gloater in advance, that's what he is." And the Nitwit Legs jumped up from the grass and ran towards the Cottage, choking with indignation.

But her abrupt movement had caused her to stumble over Duckling, who was just going to react to her hysterical remorse with an outcry eloquent enough to be heard as far as the "Pig and Whistle" when self-discipline came in with a powerful reminder that swans only raise their voices at the hour of death;

he *was* nearly dead—(Nitwit Legs had heels to her sandals)—but perhaps not quite nearly enough to justify a swan song. So he merely registered a brief strangled remonstrance, and waddled off with terrific elegance and dignity.

"Well, I've never known a duck to not move away quickly enough to avoid being trodden on."

"*Is* it a duck?" asked Holly's Legs. "It didn't quack."

"Nor it did, come to think of it. Then it must be a drake who forgot to go to the beauty parlour and get himself touched up."

The Sardonic Legs surveyed the Owner Legs with disfavour: "That bit of whimsy is worthy of our little pal who has run away to have a quiet weep over the quiet weep she's going to have when we're having our dinner at some date unspecified." He put a couple of rapid questions to the Feeding Legs, passing them on her way to the vegetable garden: "About the end of January? Good. We ought to get a decent price for them."

"Price? D'you mean you're not going to—?"

"It would choke me," sobbed the Sardonic Legs, in callous imitation. But the odd thing was that he meant it. Hens, yes, every time; geese, yes; they were decorative but not lovable, with unpleasant hissing habits. Ducks?

Somehow the ducks were different from all the rest of the livestock.

Which was exactly what Duckling yearned for him to say, only not in the plural.

The Riding Legs approached cautiously; then showed relief when he saw the Nitwit Legs was not with them. The Feeding Legs was out of the way too, gathering scarlet runners in the vegetable garden beyond the apple trees. The Riding Legs held that certain inevitable duties were better carried out without feminine fuss and tears; so with an apology to the Owner Legs and Holly's Legs, he said something in a low voice to the Sardonic Legs, who replied "Oh" . . . and stared hard for a moment at nothing. Then got up and walked back to the Cottage and round to the front door with the Riding Legs.

Unluckily, however, for all this display of masculine efficiency without tenderness, there were windows directly over the front porch and the short garden path to the gate. Tony had been quietly browsing among the fishbones in the kitchen, and so was captured easily enough, and from beneath the lid of a closed basket was already raising Cain as he was carried down the path to the Vet Legs' car; which would not have mattered, only the Nitwit Legs heard and came to her bedroom window; and when she saw what those cruel men were doing, her wails mingled with Tony's.

"Oh, my darling Tiger Tim! Oh, you can't be taking him away! And I'll never see him again! You didn't tell me it was to be *to-day,* just to-day of all days!"

(The Sardonic Legs said in a low voice, answering a sympathetic question from the Riding Legs: "No, it's not her birthday; any day would have been the same.")

So the Riding Legs called up reassurances that it was Tony, not Tiger Tim, and that there was no cause for grief, no need for tears: Tony would be back to-morrow, none the worse outwardly and ready for his dinner, when that which had to be done had been done.

"Oh, good; I'd forgotten."

Perfectly happy, now that she knew the Vet Legs was on no lethal mission with bag and chloroform, the Nitwit Legs went back to her letters, a trifle ashamed of her caterwaulings.

"That's OK," remarked the Riding Legs, no whit ashamed of his casuistry; "now we can look for the other one. He may take a bit of catching; but as long as the missis stays at her beans—"

"He's usually in the jungle bed."

"The jungle—?"

"The big border, with all that goldenrod which we've got to have cleared away."

And sure enough, down among the stems of the goldenrod, they espied the little thin body with its tiger markings; and without any difficulty, picked him up.

"All right, little chap, nobody's going to hurt you." The Sardonic Legs spoke the literal truth, but he hated himself and the Vet and the Government and the

116

Crisis and the whole damnable business which did not permit keeping as many kittens as there were kittens to keep. The fewer farewells the better for Tiger Tim. Holly's Legs, remembering when the same car had called for Holly, turned her head away, and refused to look. But the Owner Legs went across the lawn and made a suggestion, a foolish suggestion:

". . . with the cream left on."

"All right. But don't blame me if our whimsy lass smells a rat and comes downstairs."

The Riding Legs thought the delay a mistake, and said so. Nevertheless, he himself took the bottle of milk from the frig., and poured out a generous saucerful. Tiger Tim simply could not believe what lovely things were happening to him and him alone; caresses and soft words and a creamy banquet. . . . He splashed and wallowed and lapped, and no one came to oust him, and the Legs stood round and patiently waited. "They're beginning to love me. They really and truly are," thought Tiger Tim, happily.

The Nitwit Legs had finished one long letter and begun another, when she heard steps to the gate, the car door banged, the engine started up. Her subconscious nudged her:

"There's the car taking Tony away."

"Yes, I know, but it's quite all right."

Then it occurred to her that the car should have gone a full twenty minutes ago. If not, then why not?

With a sudden leap, it ceased to be her subconscious any more. She rushed to the window, flung it open—but too late; the car had disappeared round the bend, under the chestnuts.

"*Beasts!*" she cried out furiously. "Heartless beasts!"

The Riding Legs straddled away, but the Sardonic Legs stood his ground, albeit with no great courage.

"Oh . . . it's you."

"You've taken Tiger Tim! You've told me lies! Lies! Oh, and he'll wonder why I never said good-bye."

The basket containing Tony in a state that would presently figure on the Vet Legs' bill as "one cat altered 10/6," returned the next day.

It felt lighter than might have been expected, even considering. . . .

Neither was Tony heaving himself about inside, and clawing at the sides, furious at his confinement.

"Probably he's a bit dopy still," remarked the Sardonic Legs, raising the lid for him to jump out.

He did not jump. He stepped out, carefully , daintily, dopy still, as they had said. And it was not Tony. It was Tiger Tim.

"*Darling* Tim!" cried the Nitwit Legs.

The other two were silent.

Then: "Look here—" and were silent again.

Apparently the Nitwit Legs could take such

surprises in her stride rather more easily than any practical Legs. Mentally she always dwelt in the sort of world where one opened the basket in which Tony, large, furry and handsome, had magically dwindled into Tim.

"There must have been a mistake," muttered the Owner Legs, translating the obvious into words.

The Sardonic Legs reopened the front door, but the car had already driven off; and anyway it was not the busy Vet Legs himself who had handed in the basket, but his driver, a stupid girl.

"Then they've been and gone and done away with Tony," cried the Feeding Legs in consternation; for Tony was her favourite, and at the idea that he was no more, she started to cry; though at the same time she took Tiger Tim from the hugging arms of the Nitwit Legs and began to hug him herself, for after all a cat was a cat and you couldn't not be pleased to see him. Only she had loved Tony the most.

"Wait a minute. Let's get to the bottom of this. We'd better 'phone at once." The Sardonic Legs led the way to the sitting-room, followed by the others. "What's his number? There may still be time—"

The Nitwit Legs exclaimed in horror. "But even if there is, you couldn't—we couldn't—you couldn't send Tiger Tim back to him again; it would be mur-der—"

"No more murder now than it was yesterday. And for heaven's sake don't confuse the issue. Shut up now while I speak to him."

A conversation followed; not so brief nor business-like as might have been expected where only two cats were under discussion, one to be doctored and returned, and the other painlessly put to sleep.

When he eventually replaced the receiver, his household were still in a state of utter confusion as to what had really happened, though it had sounded as though both cats were still alive.

"There's been a fine old muddle!" the Sardonic Legs rather slurred over who had made the muddle or given the instructions. . . . He rather thought it might have been himself; though of course the actual fault lay in the reception, not the delivery.

"I'm still a bit stunned," confessed the Owner Legs. "Are we having Tony back?"

"I don't very well see how we can. It's all a bit awkward. A home has been found for Tony; a good home; a happy home; a home where there's a little invalid child who can hardly bear him out of her sight; I gather that even after twenty-four hours, Tony can't be snatched away without sheer cruelty to the kid."

"But he's *our* kitten. The Vet's got no right to give away our kitten without asking us, and then to send back Tim. Has he been done, by the way? Oh, all right. . . . I thought you might just know by sort of looking at his outside."

Whenever the Owner Legs started talking like the Nitwit Legs, the Nitwit Legs by some curious change-over, talked sense. She pointed out now that if

120

there had been confusion between the two cats, the one returned would of course be the one that had been doctored.

"Though I'd much rather you'd let him have lots more lovely kittens, just like himself," she added, returning to her old self; "and then those we don't want to keep, we'd have given back to the other people."

"What other people?"

The people who had the mother cats, of course."

"It doesn't usually work out like that."

"But—" The owner Legs turned to the Sardonic Legs and said:

"What about a spot of elucidation?"

"Tell us what happened?" asked the Feeding Legs, rejecting elucidation. "I was down picking beans. If you'd called me— He'd said he wouldn't be fetching 'em till Tuesday."

"That was it, you see. He had promised to come himself, and I'd have told him then which was which . . . But yesterday he was called in to a bad case of a cow losing its calf not far from here—and he apparently thought he might as well save the petrol and send along his great stupid lump of a driver while he himself was holding the cow's hand."

"But she couldn't possibly have mixed up Tony and Tim. They looked absolutely different. What did you tell her? You didn't leave her to guess, did you? I wish you hadn't been so frightfully considerate about sparing the women folk, and let us come out and see to it ourselves."

"She didn't get them mixed. I gather from him that the dear child is quite clear and certain: Tiger was the one to be doctored and returned to us. He was a bit surprised that we hadn't been able to find a home for Glamour Boy; because I had mentioned on the phone that we'd done our damndest and spread the offer all round the neighbourhood. There was such a hullaballoo going on"—with an accusing sidelong look at the Nitwit Legs—"from the window when I brought out Tim, that no wonder it drowned anything I was saying."

"And that," rejoined the Nitwit Legs, with all the dignity of innocence, "that is simply not true. What you called my hullaballoo was when you were putting *Tony* into the car. I didn't know Tiger had gone till he was gone."

"Hullaballoo number one and hullaballoo number two. Yes. Sorry. That *is* how it happened. The blame therefore had better go to where it really belongs, to that languid driver girl. She'd had notice to quit anyway, and was reading an ever-so-nice thriller: *The 39 Corpses,* I believe it was called. And I must have dared to interrupt her at the moment of solution. You see, each of the corpses had murdered the next corpse just before he became a corpse himself, but *who* had murdered corpse 38?"

"Darling, I don't mind who. Could you perhaps

come back to our own private particular corpse? Except that there isn't one."

"And that's how I wanted it to be all along," whispered the Nitwit Legs.

"I opened the basket, tipped in Tiger, pointed firmly and said: *"That* one to be *this, and this* one to be *that."*

"Well, if that's all you said, then no wonder—" began the Feeding Legs.

The Sardonic Legs gave it up: "The elucidation is over," he declared.

But the Nitwit Legs added a postscript: "Even if you pointed, if she wasn't attending very carefully and if both kittens were squirming and climbing over each other and getting their legs and tails mixed—anyhow darling Tiger Tim must be terribly hungry after his long journey back, and thirsty after the horrid stuff they gave him. And I'm going to give him the biggest saucer of milk he's ever had—"

"Except one," put in the Sardonic Legs. "His last saucer of milk on earth that he was given just before he left, with the cream still on."

Nevertheless the Nitwit Legs had her way; and the Feeding Legs went along to the kitchen to be able to tell Tiger he was welcome to the milk; and to relate the whole story with embellishments to the Riding Legs, whose whistle she had heard coming up the lane.

The other two strolled out into the garden. On the lawn they stopped and confronted one another.

"Well?"

"Well?"

"Well . . . I suppose as he *is* back, we might as well—"

So all along, the Legs had loved him best! With his natural habit of diffidence, Tiger could never have believed it, had he not received this final, overwhelming proof of their preference. He and Tony had gone away, but he was the one they wanted back. He was now the only cat of the Cottage, the only cat of the Garden and of the Meadow. Not of the jungle any more; he had little desire left in him to go stalking fiercely and alone in the dim deep undergrowth among the goldenrod (anyhow, he'd been getting pretty sick of it). And why should he stalk, now that there was no question of his being of the Tiger species? The Legs would not have kept him if they were growing hourly more afraid of him. He was their kitten. Their little cat. Their little well-beloved only cat. And he gave up badgering the Legs for special petting, burrowing and searching and thrusting his nose deep into the recesses of their persons with a lean hunger that nothing could appease, whenever they picked him up. He was appeased for ever and ever; lay contentedly on their knees or on their laps, placid and purring; played or dozed or rolled over onto his back on the bright sweet-smelling grass in the sunshine. In fact, gradually he grew to enjoy that more than the knees of the Legs. You only had to be sure of love, and independence followed.

Having realised that they must accept the situation, the Legs became genuinely fond of him. And when they wooed him and he sprang lightly away, they wished he were not so stand-offish.

"Now he's the Only Cat," remarked the Feeding Legs, "he gets all the tit-bits. Don't you, Tumti-toodles!"

"You've spoken a mouthful"; the Sardonic Legs gazed at the huge plateful of scraps, enough for three cats, set out for the sole survivor. "'God bless us every one, says Tiny Tim.'"

"Don't call me Tiger Tim any more, please. It isn't true; I'm just Tim."

Duckling felt terribly snubbed, although that was sincerely not Tim's intention in disclaiming any fierce jungle future. He was an honest as well as a happy little cat; and as his world had come right for him as a little cat, why continue to hope that the Legs' apparent aversion in the past to picking him up and petting him had anything to do with him as an embryo tiger? Even while he had still hoped that was the reason, it had been very poor consolation and only just better than nothing; he relinquished it without a single regret. It had been Duckling, not he, who out of kindness and a sense of companionship in a solitary universe, had supplied the castle in the air with all its extra furnishings, the rococo balconies, the flagstaffs, the castellated battlements. Teazle would have said that Duckling had been a very bad influence on her Tim.

"But it was they who called you Tiger Tim," he argued forlornly, "because of your stripes."

"Oh, lots of us have stripes like these," contentedly identifying himself with a huge unseen tribe peopling the universe beyond the Meadow. But he was the only one here at the Cottage. He licked a paw and washed his face to express his perfect well-being. "It was a kind of joke; or a mistake; I'm not sure which. You see," earnestly explaining "what they meant was not *Tiger* Tim but *Tiny* Tim. They said so."

"I don't think much of that for a name," remarked Duckling more and more disappointed in him.

Tim was not in the least revengeful, and was therefore innocent of any countercheck quarrelsome when he asked: "What do they call you?"

"It isn't what they call me now," with crushing hauteur that merely hid a bleeding heart, "it's what they're going to call me soon."

"How soon?" He was trying hard to take an interest in these vague hints and cloudy prophecies, but could not work up much interest.

"Sooner than you think."

Duckling waddled off, head held high, trying to believe that it was *he* who was deserting *Tim*.

Tim saw the Owner Legs coming out of the Cottage, carrying the post, and trotted to meet her with little purrs and brrs of welcome, his tail confidently erect at right angles to his body, an engaging crook at the tip.

But Duckling lay alone in the patch of rough untended grass and shrub that bordered the stream not far from the kitchen door, his head sunk despondently on his breast. . . . Suddenly—was he dreaming? Was his beak pillowed on a small patch of white moss-crepe instead of greyish-brownish-black as hitherto? He squinted down madly. It was! It *was!* A very small patch, but undeniably and purely white.

So it had begun.

(Ah, how swift may be the difference from glum despair to rapture! And how little do we know when either may overtake us, dash us to the ground or lift us on pinions into the blue empyrean. . . . And so forth and so on and etcetera.)

Duckling allowed himself a brief period of triumphant anticipation; and then, anxious to display himself to the Legs to hear what they might comment on his white patch, he followed the sound of voices round the corner to the Terrace, and began to strut in the sunshine.

But the Legs were all busy, going through their letters and journals. They did not notice little Stuff-and-Nonsense; in point of fact, they were getting a little too used to him. And they had with them a Visitor Legs who insisted that her birthday present to

the Sardonic Legs should be opened last of all. She had
brought it herself, for she had a large uninhibited
benevolent nature, and enjoyed being personally
thanked. So they were just opening her parcel, groaning inwardly even before they saw what it was. The
donor was wealthy and without taste, so it could be
assumed from past experience that something frightful
would emerge.

"Cor starve the crows!" muttered the Sardonic
Legs inaudibly.

The Owner Legs rushed in: "How lovely! A
SWAN!"

Duckling stopped dead, wheeled round (a process
difficult to ducklings), and tingling as from an electric
shock, took one look at what had been pulled out
from the wrappings and straw—

This, a swan?

—And stumbled away to seek obscurity in the
patch of rough untended grass and shrub that bordered
the stream not far from the kitchen door.

(Ah, how swift may be the transference from
rapture to glum despair! And how little do we know
when either may overtake us, dash us to the ground or
lift us on pinions into the blue empyrean. . . . And so
forth and so on and etcetera.)

"You can either *use* it or have it as an ornament.
William Morris said that nothing was ornamental that
was not also truly useful. But it's just as you like. He *is*

rather a lamb, isn't he?" The Tasteless Legs lapped up the hypocritical chorus of delight and admiration, that to any Legs without a protective rhinoceros skin would have sounded wholly unconvincing.

"I think I rather agree with W. Morris," said the Sardonic Legs, hoping he might thus, without betraying himself, elucidate to what exact use he might put a

large china swan, greenish-blue with vermilion clover leaves painted all over its body, and not even a receptacle for umbrellas as far as he could see.

The Owner Legs interrupted, doing her bit from an opposite angle of approach: "Oh *no,* darling, it's an ornament. You *must* keep it as an ornament. Think how it'll look in your study. . . ." (Yes, think!)—"What I adore about it," enthusiasm rising ever higher, "is that adorable locket round its neck. I ask you! A swan with a locket!" She burst into ghastly mirth.

But the Nitwit Legs, from whom one might reasonably have expected genuine paeans of praise, proved of no help at all. Unlike the other two, she could either be herself or nobody. And she did not like modernistic art. And especially she did not like this particular expression of it.

. . . One had to do something. One could not just crouch and be miserable forever. Besides, had not the Literary Gander told him that swans were white? Of course the shape was all wrong too, according to Great-grandma Hen; there ought to have been a tail spread into a gleaming fan. But even that was less important than for a swan to be white, not greenish-blue with vermilion shamrocks. Duckling was pretty certain that at no stage of his development could he achieve those shamrocks. . . .

". . . So would you perhaps mind just stepping across to have a look?"

Good-humouredly the Literary Gander assented: "I might as well." Though he still had not guessed why the funny little thing was so passionately interested.

The Legs were a little surprised at the sight of a Gander appearing at the french windows.

"Is it one of ours? I've never known them come so close before."

"There's no reason why a Gander shouldn't be matey, I suppose."

But the Tasteless Legs had begun to scream that she was afraid of geese; geese hissed; geese stuck out their long necks; geese pecked at her skirts. "Drive it away, somebody! Drive it away!"

So the Gander quietly withdrew, and rejoined Duckling round the corner.

"Did you see it?"

"Yes. A quite amusing bit of bric-a-brac," in light reassurance. "The right shape, but the wrong colour. Swans are always white."

Oh, the relief. Swans were always white. White as the little marks beginning to show on one's chest, which soon would spread. Whiteness was all.

That all-important point being settled, Duckling minded less over an alteration that had to be made in his mental vision of a swan pacing up and down a broad terrace overlooking a noble river, with its tail spread in a glittering fan. For Gander was highly disrespectful and flippant about this fabulous creature which had been produced from Grandma's fuddled memories of grandeur in early life. And Duckling made a mental note that struttings on the terrace and efforts to practise an effective spread of tail might now be given up. For the Swan that he was to become soon—quite soon—how soon now?—was snowy white and could fly unpinioned over the tree-tops of the Meadow, leaving terrestrial sorrows behind.

For several days he lived in a paradise of trembling bliss and anticipation and conceit. Let common little cats be content to forswear the tiger in them; poor-spirited, unambitious little cats. Let the ten antic on home waters, the approach to the Farm Opposite, downstream and under the bridge, now severely guarded by wire netting. How young they were! How voluble! How easily satisfied with bits of bread tossed to them from the bank! The Legs never threw bread on land, only into the water; so Duckling managed to believe that it was not really nice bread, not the sort of bread that would be given to swans.

(For want of something better to do, he quite benignly watched the squabbling and aquatic gymnastics over each flung bit of crust . . . .)

Surely it was not possible, it could not be, it would be too bad to be true, a phantom, a nightmare, a bugaboo. . . .

. . . "Look!" remarked the Owner Legs, "we were quite right; some of them are beginning to get white flecks on their throats."

"Two," the Nitwit Legs counted. "No, three."

"And little Stuff-and-Nonsense makes four."

. . . But of what use to be one among four swans?

"It's going to rain at last." The Sardonic Legs heaved a sigh of relief as he made his superfluous comment on the thunderclouds rolling up from the west, suffocating a sky that had been a vivid sterile blue for days.

"I felt a splash," the Nitwit Legs cried joyfully. For they had all had more than enough of the heat-wave; and the idea of moist grey skies, of the leaves and flowers sparkling with drops, and the parched earth flailed by the straight rods of rain, was unutterably restful; "Oo! I felt another!"

But it was not till an hour later that the trees shook in a wild gust, and the rain fell in torrents.

The Sardonic Legs almost danced across the bridge to shut the hen-house door, which had been left banging. As he strode back, his way across the bridge was impeded by little Stuff-and-Nonsense moping alone; he looked even dingier, more forlorn, more utterly hopeless than usual; while his brethren below wallowed in this new and entertaining sensation of wetness both ways.

It was partly exasperation, partly lightness of heart that impelled the Sardonic Legs to an act which had never before occurred to any of them. He felt he simply had to plant his toe under Duckling's rump and gaily shove him off the plank and into the water. . . .

"Nice weather for ducks!" he observed genially as he let himself go on the dastardly deed.

Splash!

And then ecstasy, loud and joyful *"Qua-a-a-aaack."*

So this was swimming! This was going with the stream! Oh, rapture incomparable! What could compare with it? Why had no one told her what she missed on dry land? What could ever, ever, ever be better than this?

The others received her among them, in her own element at last, indistinguishable, unidentifiable, her normal destiny fulfilled.

"Quack," said the Owner Legs. "Not much doubt about what *she* is."

The Nitwit Legs remarked enviously: "Aren't they having fun? Which is she? I can't see any more; they're all mixed up. We shall never know again."

"And that, my children," said the Sardonic Legs, "is the true fable of the Ugly Duckling who grew up to be a duck."

About the Author

BORN GLADYS BERTHA (SHE LATER ADOPTED "Bronwyn" as her middle name), in 1890, G. B. Stern grew up in England, her family moving frequently when she was young. A prodigy (she wrote her first play at age seven), she gained critical attention in 1916 when she published *Twos and Threes.* She went on to write over forty novels, several plays, short stories, and biographies, including two books about Jane Austen.

In 1938, Miss Stern ventured into the canine world with the publication of *The Ugly Dachshund.* Her humorous account of a Great Dane raised among dachshunds became a Disney movie in 1966, and has continued to delight readers today.